THIS BOOK BELONGS TO

Sophia
Timmy and
Daryell

TRADITIONAL
FAIRY
TALES

"Good morning, Little Red Riding Hood" said the wolf, in a
soft, oily way (page 26)

Red Riding Hood tripped into the room, fresh and dainty
from her walk (page 30)

TRADITIONAL FAIRY TALES

Illustrated by Margaret Tarrant

GALLERY BOOKS
An Imprint of W. H. Smith Publishers Inc.
112 Madison Avenue
New York City 10016

Gallery Books are available for bulk purchase
for sales promotions and premium use.
For details write or telephone the
Manager of Special Sales, W. H. Smith Publishers, Inc.,
112 Madison Avenue, New York, New York 10016.
(212) 532-6600

Typeset by Litho Link Ltd, Welshpool, Wales
Printed and bound in Norway

TRADITIONAL
FAIRY
TALES

CONTENTS

LIST OF ILLUSTRATIONS

GOLDILOCKS AND THE THREE BEARS

nce upon a time, in a pretty little house in the midst of a great forest there lived three bears.

The first was a Big Bear, with a big head, big paws, and a big gruff voice.

The second was a Middle-sized Bear, with a middle-sized head, a middle-sized body, and a voice that was neither very loud nor very soft.

The third was a Little Bear, with a little head, a little body, and a teeny-weeny voice between a whine and a squeak.

Now although the home of these three bears was rather rough, they had in it all the things they wanted. There was a big chair for the Big Bear to sit in, a big porridge bowl from which he could eat his breakfast, and a big bed, very strongly made, on which he could sleep at night. The Middle-sized Bear had a middle-sized porridge bowl, with a chair and a bed to match. For the Little Bear there was a nice little chair, a neat little bed, and a porridge bowl that held just enough to satisfy a little bear's appetite.

Near the house of the three bears lived a child whose name was Goldilocks. She was very pretty, with long curls of the brightest gold, that shone and glittered in the sunshine. She was round and plump, merry and light-hearted, always running and jumping about, and singing the whole day long. When Goldilocks laughed (and she was always laughing when she wasn't singing, and sometimes when she was), her laugh rang out with a clear silvery sound that was very pleasant to hear.

One day she ran off into the woods to gather flowers. When she had gone some way, she began to make wreaths and garlands of wild roses and honeysuckle, and scarcely thought at all of where she was going or of how she was to get back.

At last she came to a part of the forest where there was an open space in which no trees grew. There was a kind of pathway trampled or stamped across it, as if some one with broad heavy feet walked there every day.

Following this for a short distance she came, much to her surprise, to a funny little house made of wood. There was a hole in the wall of the house and Goldilocks peeped through to see if anyone was at home. She stood on tiptoe and strained her eyes till they ached; but the house seemed quite empty. The longer she peeped, the more she wanted to know who lived in this funny little house, and what kind of people they were, and, if the truth must be told, a good many other little girls would have been just as inquisitive.

At last her wish to see the inside of the house became so strong that she could resist no longer. There seemed to be someone pushing her forward, while a voice called in her ear, "Go in, Goldilocks, go in." So, after a little more peeping, she opened the door very softly, and timidly walked right in.

But where were the bears at this time? Why were they not there to welcome their pretty little guest?

Every morning they used to get up early – wise bears as they were – and when the Middle-sized Bear, who was also the Mummy Bear, had cooked the porridge she would say, if it was a fine morning:

"The porridge is too hot to eat just yet. We will go for a little walk, my dears, the fresh air will give us an appetite, and when we come back the porridge will be just right." And that is why the bears were not at home when Goldilocks walked into their house.

When she came inside the house and looked around Goldilocks was surprised to see a big porridge bowl, a middle-sized porridge bowl, and a little porridge bowl all standing on the table.

"Some of the people who live here must eat a good deal more than the others," she thought. "Whoever can want all the porridge that is in the big bowl? It looks very good. I wonder whether it is sweetened with sugar, or if they put salt into it. I'll just try a taste."

So she put the great spoon into the big bowl, and ladled out some of the Big Bear's breakfast.

Now there was so much porridge in the Big Bear's bowl that it kept hot longer than the porridge in the middle-sized bowl and in the little bowl. When Goldilocks put the big spoon into her mouth – or rather as much of it as she could get in – she drew back with a scream and danced with pain. For the porridge was very, very hot and burned her mouth, and Goldilocks did not like it at all.

"Whatever sort of person can eat such stuff?" she said.

So she tried the middle-size bowl; and you may be sure she took good care to blow on the spoon before it went into her mouth. But she need not have been so careful, for the porridge was quite cold and sticky. So she stuck the spoon upright in the bowl, and wondered again whoever could eat such stuff.

Then she tried the little porridge bowl; and the

porridge in that was just right, neither too hot nor too cold, and with just the right amount of sugar.

Having finished the first spoonful, Goldilocks thought she would try a second; and then, being still hungry, she had a third and a fourth and a fifth. By this time she could see the bottom of the bowl, so she thought she might as well look around for a comfortable chair in which to sit and finish all that was left.

First she scrambled up into the Big Bear's chair. It was cold and hard and much too high for her. Next she tried the Middle-sized Bear's chair, but that was just as bad the other way, too soft and bulging.

Then she caught sight of the teeny-weeny chair that belonged to the Little Bear. It creaked beneath her weight, but was just as comfy as a chair could be. So she sat in it and finished up the very last spoonful of porridge.

Then she began to feel very tired and sleepy and gave a great yawn. There was a crack, a groan, and a crash, and down went the bottom of the chair, for you see it was only made for a little bear to sit in.

Goldilocks felt a little frightened when she found herself on the floor, but soon got up, and, still being very sleepy, thought she would go upstairs and see if there was a bed to rest on.

A ladder stood in the middle of the room, and there was a hole in the ceiling above it. Goldilocks climbed the ladder and found, as she expected, that it led to the bedroom. It was a pretty little room, with pink and red roses peeping in at the open window, and in the middle were three beds – a big one, a middle-sized one, and a teeny-weeny one.

"They must be funny people in this house," she thought, "to have all their things of such different sizes!" She looked at the beds to see which she should rest upon, and tried the big bed first. It would not do at all – the pillow was hard and so big that it kept her head too high. The middle-sized bed was no better – it was so soft that she flopped right down in it. Then Goldilocks tried the little bed and that was just right – sweet and dainty, very white and very soft, with snowy sheets, a blue and white quilt, and a pillow exactly the right height. Goldilocks laid herself down, with her pretty head on the comfy pillow, and in a very few seconds fell fast asleep.

But before she dropped off to sleep, Goldilocks wondered for a while what the people of the house, who owned the porridge bowls, and the chairs, and the beds, would say if they knew she was there and what she had done.

Soon – very soon – there were sounds in the room

below. A big heavy foot went bump – bump – bump; a middle-sized foot went tramp – tramp – tramp; and a tiny little foot went pit-pat – pit-pat – pit-pat. The three bears had come home to breakfast! And directly they came into the room they all three sniffed and sniffed and sniffed.

When the Big Bear came to his porridge bowl, and found that some was missing, he knew at once that someone had meddled with it. So he gave an angry roar and growled in his big voice:

"SOMEBODY HAS BEEN AT MY POR-RIDGE!"

At this the Middle-sized Bear ran across the room to look at her breakfast; and when she found the spoon sticking up in her porridge bowl, she cried out, though not so loudly as the Big Bear had done:

"SOMEBODY HAS BEEN AT MY PORRIDGE!"

Then the Little Bear ran to his porridge bowl; and when he found all his porridge gone, and not even enough left for the spoon to stand upright in, he squeaked in a poor piteous little voice:

"Somebody has been at my porridge, and has eaten it all up!"

He tilted up his little porridge bowl to show the others, stuffed his little forepaws into his eyes, and began to cry.

While the Little Bear cried, the Big Bear looked round and caught sight of his chair, on which Goldilocks had left the cushion all awry. This made him angrier still, and he growled:

"SOMEBODY HAS BEEN SITTING IN MY CHAIR!"

Then the Middle-sized Bear noticed that in the soft cushion of her chair was a hollow where Goldilocks had sat down. So she called out in her middle-sized voice:

"SOMEBODY HAS BEEN SITTING IN MY CHAIR!

The Little Bear stopped crying for a moment and looked at his chair. Then he forgot all about the porridge, and called out in his squeaky little voice:

"Somebody has been sitting in my chair, and has pushed the bottom out of it!"

The three Bears all looked at one another in surprise. Whoever could have dared to do such things – in their house too!

"Some human has been here," said the Big Bear.

"Yes," said the Middle-sized Bear, sniffing around. "Let's go upstairs."

So the Big Bear went stumping up the ladder, with the Middle-sized Bear at his heels and the Little Bear last of all.

Goldilocks had tumbled the Big Bear's bolster in

"Somebody has been eating my porridge," squeaked the
Little Bear

"Somebody has been lying on my bed!" squealed the
Little Bear

trying to make it low enough for her head. The Big Bear noticed it at once, and growled:

"SOMEBODY HAS BEEN LYING IN MY BED!"

And the Middle-sized Bear said in her middle-sized voice:

"SOMEBODY HAS BEEN LYING IN MY BED!"

Then the Little Bear saw something that made all the hair on his body stand on end.

There was the bed, all smooth and white; the quilt was in its place and the pillow too; but on them, fast asleep, lay little Goldilocks. To make quite sure, he climbed on the end of the bed and looked over the rail. Then:

"Somebody has been lying on my bed!" squealed the Little Bear, *"and she's lying on it still!"*

The Big Bear, the Middle-sized Bear and the Little Bear all stood with their mouths wide open, staring in surprise at Goldilocks. Then the Big Bear gave a growl; and the Middle-sized Bear gave a grunt; and the Little Bear, who loved his little bed very much because it was so comfy, cried and cried and cried, and thought perhaps he would never be able to sleep on it any more.

The noise startled Goldilocks from her sleep. Up she jumped, and if she had wondered at seeing the three porridge bowls, and the three chairs, and the three beds, you can fancy her surprise when she saw the Big Bear, and the Middle-sized Bear, and the Little Bear.

They all came forward at the same time, and Goldilocks, terribly frightened, sprang from the teeny-weeny bed and with a single bound jumped clean through the open window.

She was lucky enough to fall on a nice soft bed of earth that the Big Bear had just dug. On and on she ran, through the forest, thinking every moment that she heard the bears sniffing behind her.

But if she could only have heard what the Bears said she would not have been at all frightened.

"I think she was rather a nice girl," said the Big Bear in his big voice.

"So do I," said the Middle-sized Bear in her middle-sized voice.

"And so do I," said the Little Bear in his teeny-weeny voice, "and I wished she had stayed to play with me."

LITTLE RED RIDING HOOD

nce upon a time there stood a pretty village of neat little cottages, with gardens bright with flowers, and beautiful cornfields all around. In this village lived a woman who had a pretty little daughter with large dark eyes and long hair falling in golden curls all over her neck. Her cheeks were as rosy as two ripe peaches, her laugh the merriest you would hear on a summer's day; but, best of all, she was kind and had a gentle heart and a helpful manner.

Everyone who knew her liked her; but those who loved her most were her mother and an old, old lady, her grandmother. To show how much she loved the child her granny made her a beautiful cloak of red cloth, with a hood to pull over her head, such as ladies wore when they rode along the highway in their grand coaches. The little girl looked very nice indeed when she wore this cloak and hood, and as the people in her street saw her tripping along, as bright as the sunshine itself, they would say, "Here comes Little

Red Riding Hood."

But the poor old grandmother fell sick, and could not go out as usual, but had to lie all alone in bed. And, as some of you know, it is very dreary to be in bed alone and ill. So the mother, who had been baking some cakes, said to Little Red Riding Hood, "Your grandmother is ill, and I want you to take her a little present. We will find a basket, and put a clean cloth in it, and you shall carry her some of these cakes and a pot of butter."

Nothing pleased Little Red Riding Hood more than to be able to make herself useful to others, but she was specially glad to do something to help her kind grandmother. She was soon ready, and her mother gave her the butter and the little cakes.

It was not a very great way from Little Red Riding Hood's home to the village where her grandmother lived; so her mother thought she might safely send the girl alone. However, she was careful to warn her not to walk slowly, and to be sure to be home before sunset.

Some woodmen were at work in the forest, cutting down the great fir trees for firewood. Little Red Riding Hood was not in the least afraid of them, for she knew they would not harm her. But soon after passing them she met a great, gaunt, hungry wolf.

This cruel animal was more savage than usual, for he had been without his dinner for two days: on the first he had paid a visit to a sheepfold, thinking he would like lamb for dinner, and the watchdog had caught him and bitten him; on the second day he had ventured to look in at a butcher's shop, where some tempting beefsteaks were hanging; but the butcher had caught him, and the wolf shuddered as he thought of the thrashing he had received.

Master Grizzly was trotting along, with a cunning, crafty look, determined to take advantage of anything that should come his way, providing it looked good to eat, when who should he see but pretty, tasty Little Red Riding Hood.

Now, the wolf would have liked to spring at the little girl and begin eating her at once; but the woodmen were near, and he could distinctly hear their blows resounding through the wood, reminding him painfully of the butcher's stick. So, like the coward he was, he pretended to be quite different from his real self.

He walked daintily up to Little Red Riding Hood, wagging his head to and fro, nodding and simpering, and trying his best to look kind and innocent. On the whole he succeeded very well; only his eyes were dreadfully green, and glared in a hungry manner;

and when he smiled he showed all the great white teeth in his jaws. But Little Red Riding Hood felt no fear: innocent herself, she was not suspicious of others.

"Good morning, Little Red Riding Hood," said the wolf, in a soft, oily way.

"Good morning, Master Wolf," answered the child.

"Pray where are you going so early?" asked the wolf, grinning and fawning, and looking more hungry than ever.

"To my granny's," replied Red Riding Hood, wondering why the wolf was so curious.

"And what have you in that basket, little girl?" asked the wolf. He sniffed and snuffed at the basket, while his mouth and eyes both watered together.

"Some cakes and a pot of butter," answered the child; and she drew back, thinking that for such a soft-spoken gentleman the wolf had rather rude habits.

"For your granny? The dear old lady! And pray where does she live?" asked the wolf, pretending to take the greatest interest in the matter.

"Beyond the hill", answered innocent Little Red Riding Hood; "she lives at the first house you come to."

"Well," said the wolf, "I don't mind if I go to see her as well: she will be pleased to see me, I know, the dear soul! and I am very fond of her" (you can't think how hungry he looked just then); "so you take this path to the right, and I'll take the one to the left, and we'll see who gets there first."

Now the cunning wolf knew very well he was certain to get to the house first, for he had chosen the shortest way. Not only that, but he also had a very certain idea of the wicked thing he was going to do when he got there, and it was a great pity Little Red Riding Hood had spoken to him at all, and let him know where her poor helpless granny lived.

While Red Riding Hood could see him, the wolf trotted meekly along, quite at his ease; but as soon as the child was out of sight, he galloped as hard as he could.

Little Red Riding Hood stopped by the way to pick flowers and make a bouquet for her grandmother. She stopped every now and then to sing in her lighthearted way; now chasing a butterfly, now searching around for wild strawberries.

Meanwhile the wolf reached the grandmother's cottage. He never stopped to gather flowers or to sing; his only thought was of dinner; and, sad to say, he thought of dinner and the grandmother together.

At the cottage he stopped a moment to catch his breath after his run; then he knocked at the door, giving two little taps, as Red Riding Hood herself might have done.

"Who's there?" cried the feeble voice of the old dame from within.

"It is your granddaughter, Little Red Riding Hood," answered the wolf; but his voice was husky, and he was out of breath with running, and the old grandmother was deaf, so she did not understand him very well.

"Who's there?" cried the feeble voice of the old grandmother again.

"Your granddaughter, Little Red Riding Hood," replied the wolf. He took great pains to imitate the child's voice, but did not succeed very well. "I have brought you some cakes and a pot of butter from my mother."

The old grandmother, as she lay ill in bed, thought her grandchild must have a very bad cold to make her speak in that strange, croaky voice, but answered:

"Turn the key and the door will open."

The wolf did as he was bid without a moment's delay, and rushed into the poor woman's room; he was so hungry that he gobbled her up, skin and bone, as easily as a spider would eat a fly. In five minutes there was not a bit of the old lady left, except a wig of false curls she had worn under her nightcap. But the wolf was only half satisfied, and began to long for the arrival of Little Red Riding Hood.

Having carefully shut the door, the wicked rascal dressed himself in the grandmother's frilled nightcap and shawl, and took her place in the bed. He pulled the nightcap well down, and drew the bedclothes well up, so as to show as little as possible of his great hairy face and body. There he lay waiting, his green eyes glaring at the door, and his mouth watering as before.

He had not long to wait before Little Red Riding Hood came, but to the greedy wolf each minute seemed an hour. At last he heard her light footsteps outside the door, and there came a gentle "tap – tap – tap!"

"Who's there?" asked the wolf eagerly – so eagerly, indeed, that he forgot to soften his voice, and set Little Red Riding Hood thinking what a bad cold her granny must have to make her so croaky. But she never suspected the truth, and replied:

"It is your grandchild, Little Red Riding Hood. I have brought a basket of cakes and a pot of butter from mother."

This time the wolf softened his harsh voice as much as he could, and said:

"Turn the key, my dear, and the door will open."

Little Red Riding Hood did as she was told, giving the door a light press, as she had often done before. As soon as she had pushed, the door stood open and she could see right into the room, with its white curtained bed, and what looked like an old lady snugly tucked up under the patchwork quilt.

No thought of the wolf was in her mind as she stepped into the room, fresh and rosy from her walk, her little basket on one arm, a great bouquet of wild flowers in the other hand.

Now, Little Red Riding Hood had never seen her grandmother except when up and dressed in her day clothes. She was, therefore, greatly surprised to see how funny the old lady looked as she lay tucked up in bed, her face nearly hidden by the frilled nightcap and the bedclothes.

"Whatever can have made grandmama's eyes so green?" she thought, as she stepped forward timidly to show the old lady the cakes.

You can fancy what a tiny mouthful a small cake appeared to the wicked creature in the bed. You might as well offer thin bread and butter to a shark. But the cunning brute was too wily to let the child see this: he simply took a cake, and nibbled it slowly, with the air of a person whose appetite was delicate.

Presently the pretend grandmother appeared to be very ill with spasms, and moaned and kicked terribly under the bedclothes. Little Red Riding Hood, very alarmed, asked what she could do to ease the pain, and the wolf, in a feeble voice, said, "Get into bed with your granny. I am too ill to get up and talk to you, dearie!"

To please her, Little Red Riding Hood began to undress, though she was rather surprised at being told to go to bed in broad daylight. But as she undid her cloak she could not help being puzzled again that her granny should look so strange and different.

"Granny," she said, "what great, rough arms you have!"

"The better to hug you, my dear," said the wolf in a squeaky voice.

"But, granny, what big ears you have!"

"The better to hear what you say, my dear," came the voice from the bed.

"But, granny, what fierce green eyes you have!"

"The better to see you with, my dear!" said the wolf, throwing off the nightcap and grinning so that the child could see right down his throat.

"But what a big mouth you have, and what large,

ugly teeth!"

"The better to gobble you up!" snarled the wolf, and, throwing off the clothes, he sprang from the bed.

Poor Little Red Riding Hood, realizing her danger at last, shrieked and shrieked and ran to the farthest corner of the room.

The wolf dashed after her, and she would soon have shared the fate of her granny; but at that moment the door was pushed open, and in burst one of the woodmen she had passed as she came through the forest.

Noticing that she had not returned, and fearing the tricks of the wicked wolf, he had hastened after her and was only just in time.

Down came his great axe on the wolf's head. A single blow from that strong arm was enough, and Little Red Riding Hood was saved.

Afterwards the brave woodman took her home, and when the story had been told you can fancy how pleased her mother was to hold her in her arms. As for Red Riding Hood, she soon ceased to be "little," but never afterwards did she speak to a wolf or any other stranger that she met on her walks.

THE SLEEPING BEAUTY

nce upon a time there lived a King and Queen, who loved each other tenderly. The only drawback to their happiness was that they had no children; so when, after many years, a little daughter came to them you may be sure there were great celebrations.

It was a beautiful little baby, with blue eyes and a fair skin; and it scarcely ever cried. The King and Queen were so pleased that they ordered a large sum of money to be given to the poor; and great preparations were at once made for the christening. Every fairy in the land was invited to act as a godmother to the little Princess, for her fond parents thought the fairies would be sure to shower gifts and graces upon her, as was the custom of fairies in those days.

But in sending out the cards of invitation a great mistake was made. One old fairy, with a nasty temper, who was really a witch, was by accident left out. She had been in another land, and the King's secretary did not know she had returned, or he would certainly have been on the safe side and sent her an invitation.

When the christening was over, all the guests passed into the great hall, where a splendid feast was served. The King and Queen made every effort to please their guests. Each of the seven fairies who had come as godmothers was provided with a plate of pure gold to eat from, and a case containing a knife, fork, and spoon, decorated with rubies and emeralds, as a token of respect and gratitude.

The feast had only just begun when the cross old fairy came hobbling in, and in a sulky tone desired that room should be made for her among the other fairies. This was done at once, and she sat down to the table. But, as she had not been invited or expected, no gold plate or decorated knife and fork had been provided for her. When she was served and saw that her things were not so good and costly as those set before the other fairies, she fell into a great rage and began muttering between her teeth that she would be revenged.

Luckily, one of the fairies noticed these angry looks, and, knowing the old witch's character, felt sure she would cast some wicked spell over the innocent little baby. So when the feast was over, this good fairy hid herself behind the tapestry hangings of the hall, so that when the other fairies offered their gifts to the Princess she might come last, and avert any mischief the old witch might try to do.

As she stood there, the good fairy heard the other fairies talking about the little child: one said what pretty eyes she had; another admired her fat little hands, and another her soft brown hair. And all the while the wicked old witch stood apart, muttering to herself.

When the time came, the fairies went forward and bestowed their gifts and good wishes on the little baby Princess. The first promised her beauty, the second cleverness, the third sweetness of temper, and so on until each had given her some good quality. Then it came to the turn of the wicked old witch to speak.

She walked into the middle of the hall, and stretching out her hand and shaking her head spitefully, exclaimed, "My gift to the Princess is that she shall prick her finger with a spindle and die of the wound."

All who heard were surprised and horrified at this wicked wish, and stood looking at the fairy, unable to believe she could be speaking the truth. Once more she stretched out her hand and, pointing to the baby

Princess, repeated her words. Then, with a screech of laughter and a look of the deadliest spite, she vanished.

Everyone, from the King on the throne to the kitchen maid who peeped behind the door, felt inclined to weep as they realized the terrible fate in store for the babe. However, at this moment the good fairy stepped from behind the tapestry and said in a gentle voice:

"Do not grieve, good friends, for things are not so bad as you imagine. The old fairy has spoken in hate and malice; but I can partly avert the effect of her anger, though not completely. Your daughter shall indeed pierce her hand with a spindle," she continued, turning to the King and Queen "but she shall not die of the wound: she shall only be cast into a deep sleep. For a hundred years she will be insensible to everything around her, but at the appointed time the appointed person will come to wake her." When the good fairy had spoken she and her sisters vanished, and the christening party broke up in sadness.

The King and Queen took great pains with the education of their little daughter, and as she grew the effects of the fairy gifts were seen by all. Every day she became more beautiful and more clever; and,

All the fairies in the land came to the christening

There lay the Princess, looking as if she had gone to sleep but
an hour before

what was of even greater consequence, she was so kind and gentle that everyone loved and admired her.

Nurses and governesses had no trouble with her, and even the great gruff house dog, who lived in the kennel in the castle yard, and who barked at everyone else, would snigger and wag his tail, and tumble with delight as soon as the little Princess came in view. He would let her put garlands of flowers round his neck, and the more she pulled his ears the better he was pleased.

Remembering what the witch had said, the King was careful to have every spindle in the palace destroyed, and forbade all his servants and subjects, under pain of instant death, to use one. Nobody was even to utter the word "spindle".

But, as you will shortly see, all this care was useless.

One day, when the Princess was just fifteen years old, the King and Queen left the palace almost for the first time since the birth of their daughter. Generally they preferred to stay at home, entertaining their lords and ladies, and the foreign guests who came to see them, in their own palace, as a king and queen ought to do. But on this occasion it happened that they were both compelled to go from home and would be absent for a day or two on important affairs of state.

The Princess, left to herself, was rather at a loss to know how to spend the time. Having tired of books and music, and being in a restless mood, she thought she would explore the castle, and especially have a look at some of the little rooms and corners she had never seen before. Thus she came at last to the most ancient tower of the castle and, climbing by the dusty stairs to the top floor, she came to a little room. Pushing open the door, which hung on a rusty and creaking hinge, she stopped in amazement. Seated on a low, old-fashioned stool in a corner of the room, and humming a tune in a funny, cracked voice, was an old woman, spinning with a spindle. The poor old creature had been allowed for years to live in this turret-room; and as she seldom left it, except to go to the royal kitchen to fetch the leftover food that was allowed her, and as she was also very deaf, she had never heard of the King's edict, and did not know that the Princess was never to be allowed near a spindle.

"What are you doing, goody?" asked the Princess.

"I am spinning, pretty lady," was the reply, when at last the old dame understood the question.

"How pretty it looks!" said the Princess; "I wish I

could spin too – will you let me try?"

The old dame of course had no idea that her visitor was the Princess, and at once she consented. The Princess took the spindle but, never having handled such a thing before, was so awkward that in a moment she had pricked her finger. At once the fairy spell began to work. The Princess looked at her wound, uttered a little scream, and fell into a deep sleep.

The old woman, much alarmed, called lustily for help, and in a few moments the ladies-in-waiting and many of the servants came running up the stairs. When they learned what had happened there was a great commotion. One loosened the Princess's dress; another sprinkled cold water on her face; another tried to revive her by rubbing her hands; and a fourth wetted her temples with scent. But all their efforts were in vain.

There lay the Princess, beautiful as an angel, the pink still in her lips and cheeks, and her bosom heaving, but her eyes fast closed in a death-like sleep.

When the King and Queen came home they saw at once that there was no remedy but patience. The wicked fairy's curse had come true. But they did not entirely despair, for they remembered also what the good fairy had said, and knew that although they themselves would probably never again see their beloved child awake, she was not really dead.

The King gave orders that his daughter should be laid on a magnificent couch, covered with velvet and embroidery, in the best room of the palace, and that guards should be stationed at the door night and day.

Feeling too sorrowful to remain in the palace, the King and Queen then went away to a distant part of the Kingdom.

The very next day the good fairy, who was thousands of leagues away, heard of her godchild's misfortune, and rushed to the palace in her chariot, drawn by fiery dragons.

Invisible to all, she passed through the palace, touching every living thing with her wand as she went. Immediately a deep sleep fell on all she touched. Ladies-in-waiting, maids, officers, gentlemen-in-waiting, cooks, kitchen maids, guards, pages, porters, even the very horses in the stables and the cats in front of the fires – fell asleep; and the strangest circumstance was that they all went to sleep in a moment, without having time to finish what they were about. The very spits before the kitchen fire ceased turning the meat when they were only half way around, and the Princess's little lap-dog stood on only three legs.

In a few days a thick and thorny hedge grew up all around the place, and the forest trees intertwined their branches to form a wall that neither man nor beast could get through.

A hundred years is a very long time, and many things happen as the days roll on. The King died, and the Queen died, and, as they had no other children, the throne passed to another branch of the royal family. As year succeeded year the very existence of the castle was forgotten, except that now and then one peasant would tell another the tale of the christening of the beautiful Princess, to which all the great lords and ladies had been invited, and the fairies too; and how the Princess had vanished, no one knew where, but was supposed to be lying asleep, on a bed of gold and silver, in a wonderful enchanted castle somewhere in the woods.

At last a century passed away.

One day the son of the reigning King was hunting in the woods, and went deeper into the forest than usual. Fancying he saw the turrets of a castle at a distance above the trees, he questioned his attendants, but they could tell him nothing. On passing through a nearby village he ordered his servants to make inquiries; but either the people knew nothing about the castle, or they were unwilling to tell. At last a very old peasant came forward and told the Prince the story of the enchanted palace. "My father," he added, "told it to me when a boy, full fifty years ago. He said the people used often to talk of it when I was little. He said all the people in the castle had disappeared on a certain day, and the castle itself was lost to view; for the woods was too thick for anyone to get through; and it was said no one could enter till the appointed time. My father himself was young when it occurred, so that, to my thinking, the hundred years have nearly passed."

These words of the old man set the Prince thinking deeply. He was fond of adventure, as most young princes are; and the more he thought about it, the more convinced he felt that it fell on him to solve the mystery. He went to sleep that night determined to try his fortune on the morrow.

Early next morning the Prince set out alone on his adventure. When he reached the woods he sprang from his horse and drew his sword to cut a path through the thick undergrowth. To his surprise, the branches gave way, and the brambles and thorns opened a passage as he proceeded. He noticed, however, that they closed behind him as thick as ever. Greatly wondering, he went on bravely till he reached the castle gate.

Here a company of musicians had been playing, and the King's fool, in his suit of patchwork, had been listening. All were fast asleep, and a man who had been singing had not even had time to shut his mouth.

Inside the gateway a hunting party had just arrived. All seemed to have turned to stone as they had ridden into the yard. Some had alighted, others were still in the saddle, but all of them were fast asleep, men and horses and dogs.

A little farther on sat a court lady and a knight. The knight had been amusing himself and the lady with a tame raven. A page stood by them with refreshments on a tray, but these were still untouched.

What struck the Prince as much as anything was the deathly silence. Not a voice spoke, not a leaf stirred, the very air seemed to be motionless.

He went on through the lower or basement floor. A groom stood fast asleep, his ear at a keyhole, a sly look of wisdom on his face.

The next room through which the Prince passed was the butler's. He had been stopped by the fairy's touch while in the very act of taking a glass of his master's choicest wine.

In another room was a kitchen maid, fast asleep,

with a dish she had been wiping a hundred years before in her hand; by her fat and lazy appearance, the Prince thought it was perhaps not an uncommon occurrence for her to fall asleep over her work.

In the servants' hall the footmen and grooms were all fast asleep. One sat behind the door: he had been pulling on his boots when the fairy threw him into the enchanted sleep, and there he sat with one boot off and the other one on. In the great kitchen the chief cook sat in a chair before the fire, with the fat skimmer in one hand and a crust in the other. One bite he had taken out of his crust, then sleep had come upon him, and he sat there, the very picture of contentment and repose. Never was there such a sleepy household since Kings first kept castles and had servants to attend them.

A dozen or more turnspit dogs, little fellows with long bodies and short legs, had been employed in turning the wheel which kept the joints of meat and poultry moving round and round, as they roasted before the fire; but not a single spit was turning, and the little dogs, one and all, were fast asleep.

In the passage, standing with his nose close to the ground, and watching intently, was the Queen's treasured cat, a Persian with a feathery tail. He had imagined, just a hundred years before, that he could smell a mouse somewhere near; and he had been waiting a hundred years for that mouse.

At the end of a long passage the Prince came to a grand staircase, and at the head of this was a tall arched doorway, with a rich velvet curtain before it. He guessed that this doorway led to some room of importance; for above the door was a great crown and two flags draped over the entrance. Here stood, too, a number of soldiers in full armour, with helmets, breast-plates, and tall spears. Very handsome and martial they looked; but each man's head had sunk upon his breast; and if the old Roman law had been put into force which pronounces death against every soldier found asleep at his post, the Princess's guards would all have been executed.

Walking past them, the Prince brushed aside the curtains, and there, on a couch in the middle of the room, lay the Princess, as fresh and sweet and blooming as any Princess could possibly be. She looked, indeed, like a rosebud in a bed of leaves, and as if she had gone to sleep but an hour before.

The Prince could not restrain his admiration. Bending over her, he looked long and earnestly; and the longer he looked, the more he admired. Then he did what most men would have done; that is to say he gave her a kiss! At least that is the general belief, but as nobody saw, and the Princess never told, we cannot be quite sure.

Instantly there was a stir and a hum all through the castle. The enchantment was broken, and, with a great sigh of relief, men, women, children and animals all woke up. Outside the Princess's room a loud clash was heard, as of armed men dressing their ranks and clattering their weapons. The fat cook in the kitchen finished the crust from which he had taken only a bite; the butler drank the glass of wine he was about to pour out a hundred years before; the kitchen maid finished wiping the dish; the groom finished pulling on his boot; the Persian cat started again to go after the mouse he had sniffed at a hundred years before; and the little dogs resumed their work of turning the spits in front of the kitchen fire.

Exactly what the Prince said to the Princess has never been told, but of course when she saw him she knew the spell had been broken, and as he was as handsome a Prince as any girl could wish for they were soon on the best of terms.

When the Prince presently appeared, leading the beautiful Princess by the hand, you may be sure the guards were wide awake. Every man among them stood at his post, his pike firmly grasped in his right hand, his head well up. The maidens of the castle threw flowers in the path of the happy pair, and there was general rejoicing.

The wedding was the grandest that had been known for a hundred years. The Princess rather hoped the good fairies would come to the ceremony, as they had come to the christening, only, as it was possible the bad fairy would come with them, no formal invitations were sent. But as the Prince and Princess lived happily together for many years, with scarcely a cross word the whole time, we may be fairly sure the fairies knew all about them and still looked after their beautiful godchild.

SNOW WHITE AND THE SEVEN DWARFS

nce, in the middle of winter, when the snowflakes were falling like feathers from the sky, a Queen sat by a window working at an embroidery frame of black ebony. As she worked and looked out at the flakes the needle pricked her finger and three drops of blood fell on the snow. And because the red blood and the white snow looked so pretty together she thought, "I wish I had a child as white as snow and as red as blood, with hair as black as this ebony frame."

Soon afterwards she had a little daughter whose complexion was as white as snow and as red as blood, and her hair as black as ebony, and she was nicknamed Snow White. Soon after the child was born the Queen died.

After about a year the King married again. His second wife was a beautiful woman, but haughty and vain, and could not bear that anyone should surpass her in beauty. She possessed a magic mirror, and when she stood before it and looked at herself she used to ask –

"Mirror, mirror on the wall,
Who is the fairest one of all?"

Then the mirror replied –

"Gracious Queen, so grand and tall,
Thou art fairest of them all."

She was satisfied, for she knew the mirror spoke the truth.

But Snow White grew, and every day became lovelier, and when she was seven years old she was far fairer than the Queen herself. One day when the Queen asked her mirror the usual question –

"Mirror, mirror on the wall,
Who is the fairest one of all?"

The answer was –

"Gracious Queen, so grand and tall,
Snow White is fairest of you all."

At this the Queen was furious, and went yellow

and green with envy. From that moment, whenever she looked at Snow White she hated the child. Day and night she could not rest for the jealousy which grew up like a weed in her breast. Then she called a huntsman and said to him, "Here, take the child out in the forest and kill her. I can bear the sight of her no longer."

The huntsman obeyed and led the child away; but when he drew his knife to pierce her innocent little heart, Snow White wept and said beseechingly –

"Oh, dear huntsman, spare my life, and I will run far into the forest and never come back."

And because she was so beautiful the huntsman had pity.

"Run away then, little one," he said, and thought, "Wild beasts will eat her, so it is all the same."

Nevertheless, he felt as if a stone had rolled from his heart, he was so relieved not to have killed her.

So the poor child wandered desolate and alone in the wide forest, and was so full of fear that she peeped behind every tree to see who was there. At last she set off running, and went over sharp stones and through thorns and brambles. She passed many wild animals, but they took no notice of her.

When she had run all day she came at evening to a tiny house and went in to rest. Inside everything was dainty and spotlessly clean. There was a wee table covered with a pure white cloth and set with seven small plates; each plate had its little spoon and knife and fork beside it, and there were seven little drinking cups. Seven little beds stood against the wall with white counterpanes.

Snow White, as she was so hungry and thirsty, ate a morsel of bread and meat from each plate and drank a little from each cup. For she did not wish to take all away from one. Afterwards, as she was so very tired, she lay down on one of the little beds. She tried them all, for some were too short and others too long, but when she came to the seventh it was exactly right. There she stayed, said her prayers, and fell asleep.

When it was dark the masters of the little house came home. They were seven dwarfs who went into the mountains to dig for metal. They lit their seven little candles, and as soon as there was light in the house saw that someone had been there and that their things were not as they had left them.

The first dwarf said, "Who has been sitting in my little chair?"

The second, "Who has been eating off my little plate?"

The third, "Who has crumbled my roll?"

The fourth, "Who has eaten some of my vegetables?"

The fifth, "Who has dirtied my fork?"

The sixth, "Who has been eating with my knife?"

The seventh, "Who has been drinking out of my cup?"

Then the first looked round and discovered a dent in his bed. "Someone has been lying on my bed," he exclaimed; and then all the others cried, "And someone has been lying in mine."

But the seventh dwarf, when he came to his bed, beheld Snow White peacefully asleep in it. He called the others and they stood round the sleeper, holding their candles over her to see her better.

"How lovely she is!" they cried. And in their delight they decided not to wake her, but to let her sleep on where she was. The seventh dwarf had to share each of his comrade's beds in turn, so they changed every hour till morning came.

At dawn Snow White woke, and felt much alarmed when she saw the dwarfs. But they were kind and friendly and asked, "What is your name?"

"Snow White," she answered.

"And how did you come here?" they enquired.

So Snow White told them how her stepmother had ordered her to be killed and the huntsman had let her

The seven dwarfs held up their candles so they could see her better

The Prince saw the glass coffin with beautiful Snow White
lying asleep

go, and how she had run the whole day till she came to their little house.

Then the dwarfs said, "If you will keep our house for us, cook the dinner, make the beds, and do the washing, sewing, and mending, and keep everything clean and in order, you can stay with us, and you shall want for nothing."

"I will do all you tell me with all my heart," said Snow White.

So she stayed with the seven little men and kept house for them while they were away in the mountains digging for gold and copper. Every evening they came home and she served up their supper. But because the little girl was left alone all day the wise dwarfs said to her, "Beware of your stepmother. She will probably find out you are here. So let no one in."

The Queen, believing that she had got rid of Snow White, thought that now she was again the most beautiful on earth and went to her mirror with the usual question –

"Mirror, mirror on the wall,
Who is the fairest one of all?"

She smiled as she waited to hear of her beauty.

The mirror answered –

"Gracious Queen, so grand and tall,
Here you are fairest among them all;
But over the hills, with the seven dwarfs old,
Lives Snow White, fairer a hundred-fold."

The Queen trembled with anger, for she knew the mirror never told a falsehood. She saw that the huntsman had deceived her and that Snow White was still alive. Now she began to ponder and ponder how she could put an end to her, for so long as she was not the most beautiful being on earth jealousy tormented her. At last she thought of a plan. Having stained her face and hands, she dressed herself like an old peddler-woman, so that it was impossible to recognize her. In this disguise she walked over the mountains to the house of the seven dwarfs, knocked at the door and called out, "Who'll buy my wares? Very cheap."

Snow White peeped from behind the window-curtains and said, "Good-day, good woman, what have you to sell?"

"All sorts of pretty things," she answered. "Beautiful stay-laces, look," and she held out one of bright floss silk.

"I may let in this good woman, surely," thought Snow White, so she unbolted the door and bought a pair of the pretty stay-laces.

"Child," said the peddler-woman, "what a figure you have! Come here and let me lace you properly."

Snow White, fearing no harm, stood to have the new silk laces fastened. The woman laced so quick and so tight that soon Snow White was unable to breathe and fell down as if dead. "Now I am fairest at last," said the woman and hurried away in great excitement at her victory.

When the dwarfs came home they were alarmed to find their dear little Snow White on the ground, not moving or speaking, as if she were dead. They lifted her and saw that she was too tightly laced. They cut the laces and at once she began to breathe again and by degrees was restored to life. When the dwarfs heard what had happened they said, "The old peddler-woman was no other than the wicked Queen. Be on your guard in future and let no one in while we are out."

The wicked Queen directly she got home went to her mirror and asked –

"Mirror, mirror on the wall,
Who is the fairest one of all?"

The glass answered as before –

"Gracious Queen, so grand and tall,
Here you are fairest among them all;
But over the hills, with the seven dwarfs old,
Lives Snow White, fairer a hundred-fold."

When she heard this all the blood rushed from her face and she was pale with fury, for she knew that Snow White was still alive.

"Never mind," she said, "I will think of a better plan this time." And, as she understood witchcraft, she made a poisonous comb. Then she dressed herself like another old woman, went over the mountains, and knocked at the door of the dwarf's house.

"Who'll buy my goods? Cheap goods," she cried.

Snow White looked out, but said, "Go away, I mustn't let anyone in."

"Ah! but you are surely allowed to look. Just see this pretty thing," said the old woman, holding the poisoned comb up to the window.

The girl admired the comb so much that she let herself be talked into buying it and opened the door.

"Come now," said the woman, "let me comb your hair properly." Poor Snow White suspected nothing and allowed the woman to do as she said, but hardly had the comb touched her hair before the poison acted and the girl fell to the ground senseless.

"You bundle of beauty," muttered the woman. "It's all up with you this time," and she went off.

Luckily, it was nearly evening and the seven dwarfs soon came home. When they found little Snow White senseless on the floor they at once suspected the stepmother had been again. Then they found the poisoned comb and directly they took it out of her hair Snow White came to herself and told them what had happened. Her friends warned her once more never to open the door to anyone in their absence.

Directly the Queen reached home she stood before her mirror and asked –

> *"Mirror, mirror on the wall,*
> *Who is the fairest one of all?"*

The glass answered as before –

> *"Gracious Queen, so grand and tall,*
> *Here you are fairest among them all;*
> *But over the hills, with the seven dwarfs old,*
> *Lives Snow White, fairer a hundred-fold."*

As the mirror said this the Queen simply shook with wrath. "Now Snow White shall die," she cried, "even if it costs me my own life."

Then she went and shut herself up in an out-of-the-way attic, where no one ever came, and made an apple that was deadly poison. Outwardly it looked so beautiful and tempting that everyone who saw it must long to taste, but whoever put the smallest morsel in his mouth was bound to die. When the apple was ready she painted her face and got herself up to look like a farmer's wife. She walked over the mountains and came to the dwelling of the seven dwarfs. When she knocked Snow White stretched her head out of the window and said:

"I mustn't let anyone in; the seven dwarfs have forbidden it."

"Never mind," said the farmer's wife, "I want to get rid of my apples. See, I will make you a present of one."

"No, thank you," said Snow White, "I mustn't take it."

"Are you afraid of poison?" said the woman. "See, I will cut it in halves; you shall have the red side and I will eat the white."

The apple was so skillfully made that only the rosy half was poisoned. Snow White longed to taste the pretty apple, and when she saw the farmer's wife eating it, she could not resist the temptation, but held out her hand and took the poisoned half. One bite and she fell dead to the ground. Then the Queen looked at her with cruel eyes, and, laughing loudly, said —

"White as snow, red as blood, black as ebony! Ha, ha! this time the dwarfs won't wake you." At home she went and stood before the mirror, and when she asked —

"Mirror, mirror on the wall,
Who is the fairest one of all?"

The mirror answered at last —

"Thou art fairest of them all."

Then the Queen's jealous heart was pacified, so far as a jealous heart can be.

The dwarfs, on coming home that evening, found Snow White on the floor not breathing and quite dead. They lifted her, looked everywhere for traces of poison, unlaced her, combed her hair, sprinkled her with water, poured some down her throat, but all in vain — the beloved child was dead and not all their efforts could restore her to life. They laid her on a bier and all seven knelt round and wept and mourned for her three days. Then they would have buried her, but she still looked so fresh and life-like, and still had such pretty red cheeks that they said, "We cannot put anything so fair in the black earth. Let us make a coffin of glass, so that she can be seen from every side, and we will inscribe on the lid, in letters of gold, her name and that she was a King's daughter. Then we will place the coffin on the mountain, and one of us will always, stay by and guard it."

This they did, and the birds came to weep for Snow White; first an owl; then a raven; then a pigeon; and then the rabbits and other wild animals.

For a long, long time, Snow White lay in the coffin and did not change. She only appeared to be asleep and was still as white as snow, as red as blood, and as black-haired as ebony.

Then it happened that a Prince wandered into the woods and sought shelter for the night in the dwarf's house. He saw the coffin on the mountain, with beautiful Snow White lying within, and read the inscription in letters of gold. Then he said to the dwarfs, "Let me have the coffin. I will give for it any sum you like to name."

But the dwarfs answered, "We would not part with it for all the gold in the world."

"Then give it to me for nothing," said the Prince. "I cannot live without looking at Snow White. I promise you I will honour and treasure her as my dearest on earth."

He spoke so earnestly that the good little dwarfs took compassion on him and made him a present of the glass coffin. The Prince had it borne away on the shoulders of his servants.

Now it happened that as they walked they stumbled over a furze-bush, and in so doing shook the poisoned piece of apple she had bitten from Snow White's throat. A minute afterwards she opened her eyes, raised the lid of the coffin, sat up quite alive and exclaimed, "Oh, dear, where am I?"

The Prince, full of joy, answered, "You are with me," and told her how the dwarfs had given him the coffin. "I love you," he went on, "better than anything in the world. Come to my father's castle and be my wife."

Snow White was willing to go with him, and they were married with great pomp and rejoicing.

JACK AND
THE BEANSTALK

here was once a widow who lived in a little country village: she was a poor lonely woman, with only one comfort to relieve the dreariness of her life; and this one comfort was her son Jack. As Jack was an only child, you can imagine how much affection was bestowed upon him – how the poor widow went without food that Jack might not feel their poverty. How she watched over him day and night. How, in fact, she loved him as only a widowed mother can.

Now, Jack was not at all a bad-hearted fellow. He was generous, helpful, and brave. He would go any distance on an errand to please a friend; he would give all he had to anyone who begged of him; and if he saw a big boy ill-treating a little one, the bully was pretty certain to receive a sound thrashing at the hands, or rather at the fists, of Jack. But he had one fault, which many brave, open-hearted lads have: he was wasteful and reckless. Not knowing the value of money, he spent it as freely as if his mother had hundreds of pounds, but she loved him so fondly that she did not like to reprove him, and allowed him as he grew up to become more and more extravagant, while every day they grew poorer and poorer.

At last, on going to her money-box one night, the widow found that there was not a shilling left. The box was empty except for one little threepenny-piece, which had been clipped all round the rim and had a large hole punched out of the middle. Then at last she began to reproach Jack.

"Oh, you heedless, wasteful boy!" said she; "see what you have brought me to with your extravagance! All I have is gone, except the threepenny-piece which no one will take, and we must have bread to eat. Nothing now remains but to sell my poor cow. When the money we get for her is gone I do not know what we shall do. Oh dear! Oh dear!"

Jack saw at last what he had done, and promised to make up for his careless ways, really meaning what he said. He declared that he would be the prop of his mother's old age; and early next morning sallied forth to sell the cow.

As he trudged along, swinging his stick, and cutting off the head of a thistle now and then for pastime, he began to think how much money he should ask for the cow, and to whom he should sell her. The more he thought about it the less he could make up his mind. Like many people in similar difficulties, he resolved to leave the matter to chance. Directly afterwards he met a butcher who asked him what he was going to do with "that thin, old cow."

"Neither thin nor old," answered Jack rather angrily, "but if you want to know, I'm going to sell her."

"Well," said the butcher, who knew Jack's easy-going temper, "I'll tell you what I'll do. You see these beans in my hat? Beautiful, aren't they? Red and blue and purple and all sorts of shades. I shouldn't offer another man so much; but you are a clever fellow and like to drive a hard bargain, so I'll give you the lot for the poor old cow."

Jack was much flattered at being called a clever fellow, and moreover liked the look of the beans. So he stupidly agreed at once with the offer made by the wily butcher, who drove off the cow, laughing up his sleeve at Jack's simplicity. The boy then turned homeward, fancying he had done a rather clever thing, and calling to his mother from afar to come out and admire what he had brought her.

When the good woman heard with her own ears and saw with her own eyes how foolishly Jack had acted, she was about as angry as anyone could be.

She had made up her mind, poor woman, what she would buy with the money the cow would fetch. She had settled where she would buy the flour for the bread, and how much she would save out of the price of the potatoes by taking a quantity at a time, and how she would manage to scrape enough together to buy a comforter for her son to wear in the winter, and perhaps something warm for herself. And then, when she had planned everything so nicely, to have that silly boy standing there with a few beans in his hand and a broad smile on his face!

The old woman quite lost patience, and, having scolded Jack for his stupidity, angrily tossed the beans out of the window, bewailing her lot in having such a careless, rattle-brained boy for a son. Jack, who was really sorry, did his best to console her, but, though they kissed and made friends, that fact did not undo his folly, and they both had to go to bed without supper.

The next morning Jack found himself awake two full hours before his usual time, and a little sprite inside him seemed to be calling, "Breakfast! breakfast! breakfast!" pinching him at the same time. He got up quickly and, as he dressed, looked out of the window. What he saw made him start with wonder and rub his eyes to make sure he was awake. Then, with an exclamation of surprise, he ran downstairs as fast as he could and into the garden.

From the corner where his mother had flung the beans rose a great thick beanstalk; not a single stalk really, but a number of stalks twined and twisted in such a way that they formed a sort of ladder. The ladder went up and up so high that the top seemed lost in the clouds. The lower part of the beanstalk was as thick as a tree trunk, and Jack tried vainly to shake it.

Now, Jack was an adventurous kind of boy, and could not pass a ladder without a desire to climb it. When he saw this great beanstalk, he at once decided to get to the top, and see "where it led to." But first, like a dutiful boy, he ran back to the house to tell his mother of his intention. She tried all she could to dissuade him, feeling sure some harm would come to him. But Jack was a headstrong boy, and, having made up his mind, not even his mother's tears could stop him. Up the beanstalk he went, his mother standing underneath, calling and threatening and pleading in vain.

Hour after hour he climbed, and the higher he got the more hungry he grew. At last, panting for breath and almost exhausted, he reached the top, and found himself in a strange country.

It was not a beautiful country by any means: not a tree, nor a shrub, nor a house, not a living creature, was anywhere to be seen. Jack found himself, in fact, in as dry a desert place as you can imagine; not at all the kind of country anyone would choose who went to seek his fortune.

Jack seated himself on a block of stone, and thought of his mother, reflecting with sorrow how he had again brought trouble on her devoted head by his lack of thought. He was also in sore trouble on his own account; he could find nothing to eat, he was woefully exhausted, and began to feel much afraid that he would die of hunger.

Still, however, he walked on, hoping to see a house where he might beg for food; but there was no sign, far or near, of anything of the kind. Suddenly, however, he became aware of a kind of cloud rolling toward him. It parted, and disclosed, to his great surprise, a beautiful lady. She was dressed in a shining robe of white, and held in her right hand a slender white wand with a peacock of pure gold at the top.

Jack stood gazing at the lady with the greatest amazement, but she approached and asked:

"How did you come here?"

Her face was kind and she smiled very pleasantly,

so Jack, after bowing low, told her about the cow and the beans and the great thick beanstalk.

She smiled still more and, to his surprise, asked:

"Do you remember your father?"

"No," he answered sadly. "My mother always weeps when I mention him and will tell me nothing."

"Listen," said the lady. "I will tell you a story of which your mother has never dared to speak. But before I begin you must give me your solemn promise that you will do exactly as I command. I am a fairy, and unless you act as I tell you, I shall not be able to assist you, and there is little doubt that, left unaided, you will not only fail in the attempt I wish you to undertake, but perish."

Jack at once promised, and the fairy continued:

"Your father was a rich man, and, what is more, had a kind heart. No one who came to him for help was ever turned away; and he would often seek out people in distress without waiting for them to come to him. Not many miles from your father's house lived a cruel giant who was the dread of the whole country. When he heard your father's goodness praised he hated him in his heart, and vowed to destroy him. To do this he came with his wife to the place where your father lived and pretended to have lost all his property by a great earthquake. Your

The cloud parted and there stood a beautiful lady, dressed in
a shining robe of white

The giant was not long in reaching the top of the beanstalk

parents received him kindly, for they were good to all. One day, when the wind was blowing loudly over the sea, the giant came to your father with a glass in his hand. 'Look through this,' he said, 'here is something that will grieve your kind heart.' Your father looked, and saw several ships in danger of going down or being driven on shore. The giant begged him to send his servants to assist these poor people, well knowing he would not refuse. All the servants, except your nurse and the porter, were at once sent, but hardly were they out of sight when the cruel giant fell upon your father and killed him.

"The cruel monster intended to kill you also; but your mother fell at his feet and begged so piteously that he agreed to spare you both on condition that your mother promised never to reveal the story. Then he set about plundering your father's house and afterward set fire to it. While he was thus employed, your mother took you, a poor weak little baby, in her arms, and fled as fast as she could. For miles and miles she carried you, in an agony of fear, dreading every moment that the cruel giant would alter his mind and come after her. At last, exerting all her strength, she reached the village in which you have lived so long. Now you know why she has never opened her lips to you on the subject of your father.

It has been a hard trial for her to see you growing up in poverty, while she knew another had grown rich on the inheritance that should have been yours. But her promise, though given to a wicked giant, was a promise after all, and she has kept it.

"It is now for you to regain the fortune your parents lost; for all this wicked giant has belongs of right to your mother and you. I have taken you under my protection, for I was your father's guardian. But fairies are bound by laws as well as mortals, and through a sad mistake I lost my power for a number of years and was unable to help your father when he most needed me. My power only returned on the day you went to sell your cow. It was through me that the butcher found the beans, and it was me that induced you to buy them and that caused the beanstalk to grow. I filled you also with the desire to climb, but now you have reached this country where the wicked giant dwells I can only help you if you are willing to help yourself. You are reckless, but, I trust, brave and earnest. Go boldly forward, fearing neither danger nor hardship. Your enemy's house – or rather your own—lies straight before you. Remember that my protection can be given to you only as long as you work boldly and faithfully."

The fairy then vanished.

Jack sat for a time in utter amazement at the wonderful things he had heard.

"Poor mother!" he thought, "how she must have suffered! Well, I will do my best to help her, and to punish this wicked giant."

Resolving thus, he continued his journey, wandering farther and farther. At last, as the shadows of evening were beginning to fall, he came in sight of a fine, spacious mansion. He went straight up to the door, and asked the women who stood there for a night's lodging and a crust of bread.

The woman looked ugly, haggard and careworn, but did not seem ill-natured. She was greatly surprised to see him, and several times motioned him to go away, as if she would gladly have been rid of him and his request together. But Jack, determined to go through with his adventure, stood his ground manfully. At length, when she saw that he paid no heed to her silent warning, she glanced sorrowfully at him and said:

"Alas! my poor boy, I dare not take you in. My husband is a mighty and cruel giant. He goes hunting every day, and brings home men to supper – not to sup with him, but to be eaten – for he feeds almost entirely on human flesh, and is out of temper when he cannot get it. He has gone out today to try and catch a fat citizen, and if he has been unsuccessful, he will make you do instead."

Jack was greatly terrified by this account of the owner of the house; the more so when he heard that the giant was expected home directly. But he was very hungry and very tired – and, besides, the fairy had told him he must be brave and bold. So he begged the good woman to take him in, just for this one night, and to hide him somewhere; and she, being a good-natured sort of person for an ogre's wife, consented.

She led him through a fine hall, furnished with chairs as big as bedsteads and cups that held a gallon; and upon one table Jack saw a large spear-head, which the woman told him was her husband's toothpick. Through other rooms they went, well furnished, but all cold and gloomy; until, at the end of a long gallery, Jack saw something that looked like a grating or the front of a cage. Behind this cage, two or three men moved to and fro, wringing their hands and weeping. They were, in fact, the giant's prisoners, whom this monster kept just as a farmer might keep turkeys and geese to kill at Christmas. Jack's blood ran cold, but he kept up his courage, and followed his hostess to the kitchen. Here was a roaring fire, and everything looked warm and comfortable. The giant's wife placed a plentiful supper on the table; and when you remember that Jack had not only eaten nothing all that day, but had gone to bed hungry the night before, you can fancy what a meal he made.

Just as he had finished supper they heard a sound like fifteen trumpets, and the woman started up in a fright, exclaiming, "My husband is coming!"

"Does your husband always have trumpets played when he comes home?" asked Jack.

"What trumpets?" asked the giant's wife. "Foolish boy, he requires no trumpets to be blown before him; the sound you hear is my husband blowing his nose."

Then there came footsteps, like fifty dray-horses walking together. Nearer and nearer they came, "tramp! tramp! tramp!" and then there was a loud knock at the door which made the house shake.

"Ah," cried the woman, "he is in a rage, I can tell. If he sees you he will kill you and me too. What shall I do?"

"Hide me in the oven," said Jack, who now somehow felt quite bold as he remembered that he would soon be face to face with his father's murderer and the cause of all his mother's troubles.

Then the woman ran and opened the door in a hurry, and the giant came stalking into the kitchen.

"I smell fresh meat!" were his first words.

It was soon evident that the giant was in a terribly bad mood, for no success had come to him that day in hunting. He had met no one but a thin man, whose flesh was not tender, and who had escaped, and an old man who had lived so long in the workhouse on dry bread and gruel that he was nothing but skin and bone, and the giant in disgust had kicked him and let him go. So he was in a very bad mood indeed, and his looks were angry.

"I smell fresh meat," he repeated.

His wife, of course, knew that he smelt Jack, but, being really anxious to save the lad, she replied, "It must be the men in the cage." Then she hastily brought her husband's supper to divert his thoughts.

The giant glanced hungrily at the food; but still he muttered to himself—

"Fee, fi, fo, fum,
I smell the flesh of an earthly man."

The business of supper soon occupied all his attention. It appeared that he was saving up the men in the cage for a treat, and Jack, peeping through a crevice in the oven, was surprised to see that his meal consisted of three legs of mutton, seven fresh loaves, and a few other trifles of the kind. This did not take long to consume, and he then leant back in his chair and, in a voice of thunder, called to his wife:

"Bring me my hen."

She at once placed on the floor before him a very fine hen.

Jack, still peeping through the crevice, at first thought the giant was going to eat this also.

"*Lay!*" roared the giant, and at once the hen laid an egg of solid gold.

"*Lay!*" cried the giant again, and the hen obediently laid another egg, larger than the first.

Meantime the wife went to bed, leaving her husband to amuse himself with the hen. In a little while, after quite a pile of golden eggs had been laid, the giant began to nod, and his hands hung limply over the arms of his chair before the fire. Then his head sank lower and lower, and at last he went fairly off to sleep, snoring like the roaring of cannon in battle. In his sleep the giant seemed to have an idea that something unusual was going on, and several times muttered, "Fee, fi, fo, fum;" but the warmth made him more and more drowsy and his snores grew louder.

Now was the time for Master Jack. Creeping silently from the oven, he stole on tip-toe across the room and snatched up the hen, now proudly strutting on her pile of golden eggs.

Thrusting the frightened bird under his arm, he went softly to the door, casting many a backward glance at the giant, who continued to snore as loudly as ever.

Finding the heavy iron bar across the door could not be lifted without noise, Jack jumped out of the window and ran off. Away he went, and at length found himself at the spot where the beanstalk reared its head through an opening like a well. Down the beanstalk Jack clambered, still clutching the precious hen; and you can fancy how pleased his anxious mother was to see him again. But she was still more pleased when Jack showed what a rich prize he had secured.

"*Lay!*" he cried, and the hen obeyed her new master as readily as she had obeyed the giant, and laid an egg every time she was told.

For some time Jack and his mother lived happily enough. The golden eggs of the hen supplied all their wants; and had it not been for what the fairy had said, Jack would not have thought any more of the beanstalk. But the more important part of his task was yet unattempted. He had indeed rescued his mother from poverty, and escaped from it himself, but that was not all he was expected to do. His father had been murdered by the giant, and murdered in a very treacherous way. The more he thought of what the beautiful lady had told him, the more it appeared to Jack that he must finish the task the fairy had set him, and that he could not rest content as long as the wicked giant lived to enjoy the riches he had acquired so unfairly.

So one day he told his mother that he must mount the beanstalk a second time. Again the good lady did all she could to dissuade him, but, owing to his promise to the fairy, Jack could not tell her his real reasons for going. At length his mother, with a heavy heart, was forced to consent.

But first, fearing that the giant's wife would know him again, he got his mother to make him a different suit of clothes, and he carefully painted his skin so he might appear as unlike his former self as possible.

Then once more, with great difficulty, he climbed the beanstalk, and, having rested awhile on the stones, made his way boldly to the giant's mansion. This time it was not such an easy matter to get in. The old dame declared that once before a poor boy had come for shelter, and had stolen her husband's prized hen, and that the giant, having forced her to confess that she had let someone in, had revenged himself by beating her cruelly. Jack felt sorry for her in a way, but he was very determined, and at last, after much persuasion, convinced her to admit him for the second time. Again he was given a good supper and again, just as he was finishing, the sound as of trumpets was heard approaching. This time Jack had no need to ask what it meant, but he thought it best to do so.

"Hide in the big cupboard," whispered the giant's wife hurriedly.

Jack was soon safely inside and was glad to find a chink through which he could see what the giant was about.

This time the giant was in a fairly good mood for he had robbed three men of a lot of money, which he had hidden in a cave by the wayside. The poor men themselves he had bound hand and foot, and left in the cave till he should call for them.

He ate his supper with great relish, and, his thoughts running on the money he had stolen, he roared to his wife to bring him his money-bags, that he might count how much he had. He was a greedy giant, and took great delight in hoarding money and counting it over and over again. The wife soon returned, dragging two heavy bags, one filled with golden sovereigns, the other with new shillings.

Snatching them from her hand, the giant gave her a box on the ear, telling her that was for her trouble.

"Now you may go to bed, you old simpleton!" he roared.

This the poor woman was glad enough to do, you may be sure.

Then the giant began to count his money, beginning with the gold sovereigns.

"One, two, three, four," — and so on. Presently he got to the hundreds – "One hundred and one – one hundred and two." By the time he got to "Five hundred and eighty-one – five hundred and eighty-two – " his head began to nod.

In another five minutes he was fast asleep. Then Jack came out of his hiding-place on tip-toe, and clutched both the bags. Just as he was making his way to the window, a little dog, that had lain unobserved under the giant's chair, jumped toward him with a shrill – "Yow! yow! yow!"

Luckily, Jack had not quite finished his supper when the giant's knock came to the door, and he had hidden a bone in his pocket. With this yelping dog to silence, a bone was the very best thing Jack could have had. The giant turned uneasily once or twice on his chair, but did not wake, and the starving dog was soon too busy with the bone to care what happened to his master.

So for a second time Jack made off with the wicked giant's treasure, and in due course arrived safely at the foot of the beanstalk.

But all was not well at home. His poor mother had done nothing but fret from the moment he went away; and so anxious had she been that she was ill – in fact, nearly dying. When she saw her boy safe and sound, however, the good woman soon recovered.

With the bags of gold the cottage was rebuilt, and for some time they lived happily together; but presently Jack felt he could stay no longer, and must try once more to penetrate the giant's abode, for his task was incomplete so long as his father's death was unavenged. This time he did not tell his mother of his intention, for he knew she would try to dissuade him, and he had made up his mind to go anyway. So, early one morning, he started on his third expedition. This time it cost him still more trouble to gain admission, for the giant's wife had grown very suspicious; but Jack was so well disguised that she did not recognise him, and he at last contrived to get inside the mansion once again.

When the giant returned from hunting he muttered furiously, "I smell fresh meat!" and began to search the room. Jack this time had hidden in the boiler, and the giant, being very hungry, did not take the trouble to lift the lid. His supper consisted of a whole salted hog and three large cod-fishes. This salt fare made him very thirsty, so he took three great casks of drink, whereas his usual custom was to wash down his supper with only two. The liquor got into his head, and put him in a very good mood. He began to sing and roared to his wife to bring his harp.

This harp was a most wonderful instrument. Directly it was placed on the table it began to play, of itself, the most beautiful music. The giant rose and began to dance. The harp presently played slower and more softly; and the giant, growing sleepy, lay down at full length on the ground and began to snore.

"Now," thought Jack, "is my time," and, slipping from his hiding-place, he seized the harp. But the harp was enchanted, and, when Jack seized it, cried "Master! master!"

Up started the giant with a roar, and away ran Jack with the harp. The giant thundered after him as fast as he could, crying:

"Oh, you villain! It was you who robbed me of my hen and of my money-bags, and now you take my harp! Wait till I catch you. I will eat you alive!"

"Do," cried Jack, "when you catch me!" For he

could see that the giant, in his tipsy condition and blind with rage, would not be able to run very fast.

Jack ran his hardest, and had got a good start of his pursuer by the time they got to the top of the beanstalk. Down the stalk Jack slid, holding the harp, which played all the time the saddest of sad music, until he called out to it sharply "Stop!" an order that was at once obeyed.

The giant was not long in reaching the top of the beanstalk, and Jack could see his great boots descending. When he reached the bottom, our hero called loudly to his mother, who was sitting weeping at the cottage door:

"Mother! Mother! a hatchet! Quick!"

Not a moment was to be lost. Jack seized the hatchet from her hands and chopped at the beanstalk with all his might. The giant lost his hold and was killed as he came crashing down with a fall that shook the earth!

Jack's mother, when she could summon courage, bent over the great body, and was astonished to recognize the cruel monster who had murdered her husband years before.

BABES IN THE WOODS

nce upon a time there lived a good and wise Lord and a beautiful Lady. They had two dear little children – a fine boy and a very pretty girl. Their home was one of the happiest in all the land, for they loved one another dearly; and the father and mother, being noble and kind, had taught their children to be so too.

But soon great misfortunes came to this happy family.

First, the mother died, which was a great blow to the children. Then, a short time after, when the boy was only five years old and the little girl a year younger, their dear father was also taken away.

When the good Lord knew that his end was near, he sent for his brother; and, calling him to the bedside, said:

"Dear brother, I am dying. In a few short hours, or days at most, my poor little Babes will be alone in the world. Happily, I am able to leave them well provided for, as I have saved money enough for all their needs. I leave them to your care, since you are the only relative they have. Guard and cherish them, I beg you, for my sake! My son in years to come will have this castle, and money enough to keep up his proper state; and my daughter will have a sufficient fortune. I ask you, my brother, to take charge of everything until they are old enough to manage their own affairs. I beg you to promise that you will deal justly by them, and love them for my sake!"

"I will care for them as if they were my own!" said the younger Lord. A few hours later the good Lord died, well content.

A week or two after the funeral the Uncle took the two children away to his own castle to live with him, and at first treated them kindly.

At heart, however, he was a bad man, and quite unlike the good Lord who had passed away. He was greedy and cruel; and while he watched the helpless children at their play a cunning plan shaped itself in his mind by which he hoped to get rid of them, and thus be able to keep their money and lands for himself.

One night, in late summer, he sent for two robbers, whom he knew to be bold and bad men, ready in return for money to do any cruel deed. He bade them take the two little children out into the forest next

The robbers started to fight, while the children sat helplessly
on a tree trunk

They brought the gold-tinted leaves in their bills and
showered them on the babes

day and kill them, promising them a large sum of money in return. The robbers agreed to do as he wished, and, very pleased at the prospect of getting money so easily, they sat drinking until late in the night.

Next morning the wicked Uncle came quite early to the room where the children slept. "Rise," he said, "and dress quickly. Two friends of mine are going to take you for a stroll in the woods this fine morning."

"But we haven't had our breakfast yet, and we're so hungry!" cried the little boy, remembering, also, that they had not had any supper the night before.

"I don't like those big, ugly men! They frighten me!" cried the little girl, when they reached the hall where the two robbers were waiting.

She began to cry, but the wicked Uncle took no notice of either tears or words. The robbers took the children by the hand and dragged them away to the darkest part of the woods.

The poor little orphans were so frightened that they dared not even whisper to each other. When they came to the darkest part of the forest, and found that the robbers meant to kill them, they cried and cried, and, falling on their knees, begged for mercy.

So piteously did they plead that one of the men, whose heart was not quite so hard as that of his mate, felt suddenly a little sorry for the cruel deed he was about to do, and would have spared their lives. But his companion would not hear of this, and cried angrily, "Do not be a fool, man! Let us kill the brats, or else we shall not get the reward!"

The other robber, however, still wished to save the children; and, at last the squabble between the two grew so fierce that they started to fight, drawing knives and rushing at each other desperately.

The two men fought for a long time, while the children sat helplessly on a tree-trunk, fearing to run away lest the cruel knives should be plunged into their own hearts.

At last the meanest robber was killed. The other then took the trembling children by the hand and led them on again. When they had reached the most lonely part of the forest, he made them sit down under a tree, and said to them, "Stay here a short time and rest, little ones, while I go to find some food for you! I will not be long!"

He soon disappeared among the trees, and quickly made his way to the path, since he had not the slightest intention of returning to the children again. When he got back to the castle of the wicked Uncle, he declared that the little boy and his sister were dead, and claimed the promised reward. The bad

Lord was glad to hear that he might now claim the estates of his dead brother, and willingly paid over the money to the robber, who took it and returned to his usual evil way of living.

Meanwhile, the poor Babes sat under the tree and patiently awaited the robber's return. After several hours had passed they felt sure he did not mean to return to them, and the little boy said:

"We are left alone, little sister, and we must try to find our way out of this dreadful forest as best we can!"

The little girl began to cry, for she was already so tired and hungry that she felt she could hardly move. Her brother took her by the hand, bravely keeping back his own tears, and together they wandered through the dense woods, trying to find a path that would take them out.

But every step they took led them farther into the forest; and at last the sun went down and night came on.

Then, as the stars came out one by one, the little girl cried:

"I can go no farther, dear brother! Oh, must we stay all night in this dreadful forest?"

"I'm afraid so, little sister!" replied the boy, adding with a brave smile, "But it is not really so dreadful, after all. See, there are the dear little stars twinkling above us."

They were now in a deep, sheltered glade, and, too hungry and worn out to go another step, they threw themselves down on a soft mossy bank. With their little arms lovingly twined round each other, and their pale cheeks closely pressed together, they soon fell asleep. Two dear little squirrels perched on the tree above stood as guards over them all night; and the sweet song of a nightingale lulled them to sleep. They dreamed of their dear father and mother; and, as the night wore on, a sweet smile of peace stole over the faces of the two little sleepers.

When dawn came and the golden sunlight streamed through the over-hanging trees, the two sweet Babes still lay locked in each other's arms. The sun climbed higher and higher, but still they did not stir nor open their eyes, for they had died in their sleep, and all their trouble were at an end.

When the robin-redbreasts and the squirrels looked down on the little brother and sister, they knew that they were dead; and as the birds could not dig a grave for them, they brought the gold-tinted leaves in their bills and showered them over the still forms which lay upon the ground.

Quickly and quietly the little workers performed

their task of love; and, very soon, the two Babes were covered with a soft pall of golden leaves. Then the robins sang a mournful song, and the squirrels and the rabbits felt so sad that they would not frisk or play any more that day.

As for the wicked Uncle, he did not long enjoy his ill-gotten gains. From that day on, no luck came to him. The robber who had left the children to die in the wood was condemned to death for another crime, and made a full confession of his misdeeds, so that the sad story of the poor Babes in the Wood was known all through the countryside. People would have nothing further to do with the wicked Uncle; little by little he lost all his ill-gotten wealth and died at last in great poverty.

BEAUTY AND THE BEAST

n a large city of the East once lived a very rich merchant, who had a splendid house and large warehouses full of costly goods; a hundred guests sat down at his table every day.

His family consisted of three sons and three daughters. The sons were tall, well-grown young men, and the daughters were all very handsome, especially the youngest. So bright and happy was her face, and so winning were her ways, that, as a child, she had been the pet of the family, and everyone had called her "Little Beauty." Now that she was a tall, grown-up girl, the name still clung to her, and this made her sisters very jealous.

The youngest daughter was not only better-looking than her sisters, but better-tempered. The sisters were very vain of their wealth and position, gave themselves many airs, and declined to visit the daughters of other merchants on the grounds that only persons of quality were fit to speak to them. Every day they went to balls, plays and parties, and made fun of Little Beauty for preferring to spend her time in reading and other useful occupations. As their father was known to be so wealthy, the two elder sisters received many offers of marriage, but they always declared that they would accept no one below the rank of duke or earl. Beauty also had many offers, though she said less about them, and always told her suitors that she thought she was too young to marry and would rather spend some years longer with her father, whom she loved dearly.

Happy indeed it was for the merchant that he loved his sons and daughters better than his wealth; for he little thought, as he sat at the head of his plentifully supplied table with his smiling guests about him, that several terrible misfortunes had happened, and that he was, in fact, no better than a ruined man. One of his largest ships, with a very costly cargo, was wrecked at sea, and only two of the sailors were saved, after clinging for days to the fragment of a mast; another equally valuable vessel was taken by pirates; and a third fell into the hands of the enemy's fleet. By land he was equally unfortunate: his largest warehouse was burned, and robbers attacked and plundered a caravan of camels conveying his goods across the desert. So, within a few months, he sank from the height of wealth to the depth of poverty and want.

Very different from their former splendid mansion was the quiet little country cottage to which the merchant and his family now moved. There were no pleasure grounds, fountains, groves of trees, or ornamental waters. The once wealthy merchant, who had employed hundreds of servants, was now reduced to toil in the fields with his sons to gain a bare living; and they had to work early and late just to make a living. Hard as their lot seemed, the three sons manfully met the reverses of fortune, and both by word and deed did all in their power to help their father.

The two elder daughters were far different, for they spent all their time fretting over their losses, and their grumbling not only made the poverty doubly hard for themselves but embittered the lot of the merchant and his sons. They would not enjoy the plain fare the others ate with relish; they rose late, and spent the days in idleness, too proud and lazy to devote themselves to any useful task, and despising their brothers for working hard.

While her two elder sisters sat crying and sobbing, Beauty would be fully employed in spinning or in seeing to the household affairs; and she always had a smile for her father and her brothers when they came in wearied from their work out in the fields.

By working hard, morning, noon and night, the merchant and his sons were fortunate to earn enough to keep them from want. In fact, in one respect the merchant was better off, for whereas during the time of his prosperity he had often been kept awake at night by anxious thoughts for the safety of his ships, his warehouses, and his stores of gold and silver, such thoughts now never entered his mind, and he slept soundly and peacefully till morning. Also his conscience was clear, for he had always been honest in his dealings, and, though everyone knew of his misfortunes, he was still respected by all whose respect was worth having.

After they had lived in this way for about a year a great change came over their quiet life. One day a messenger arrived at the merchant's cottage with an important letter. It contained news that a ship, long given up as wrecked and lost, had safely anchored in a distant port, and the merchant was needed to go and take possession without the loss of a day.

You can imagine what a stir this made in the little household. The merchant's sons looked hopeful, and the two elder sisters, radiant with smiles, began at once to discuss plans for future pleasures. Beauty was glad too; but she was chiefly glad because she loved to see her father happy. The merchant was pleased at the prospect of regaining a portion of his wealth more for his children's sake than for his own, and he had a hundred projects for giving his daughters handsome presents on his return.

Before he started, he asked each in turn what special present she would like him to bring home when he had received the money for his cargo. The two elder sisters, who had counted on this very question, were at once ready with a long list of things they wanted, mostly fine dresses and jewels; but their requests somewhat surprised and pained their father, for they seemed to think his whole fortune had been restored instead of a single vessel.

He, however, promised that they should have what they wanted if he could possible secure it. Beauty had not been thinking about herself at all, and when she heard what her sisters wanted decided that all the ship contained would not suffice to cover the cost.

"Well, Beauty," asked her father, "and what do you desire? What can I bring you my child?"

"Nothing at all, thank you, father," she replied.

But when he seemed hurt at this she kissed him and flung her arms round his neck, saying:

"Yes, dear father, there is one thing I should love. We have no flowers in our little garden here, though

I am sure it is very nice. Please bring me, if you can, a single red rose."

Beauty, indeed, had never cared for wealth, and only made this request so that she might not seem to be affronting her greedy sisters.

The sisters laughed at Beauty in secret for what they called her stupid choice; but did not dare to say so openly, for fear of their brothers.

The merchant rode off on a horse he had borrowed from a friend. The three daughters stood at the door, waving their handkerchiefs, and crying "Good-bye!" But it was Beauty who got the last kiss.

The merchant's journey was not so prosperous as he had hoped. The cargo, indeed, had been saved, and the ship was safe in port; but a lawsuit had ensued, and there was so much to pay that the merchant set out for home not much richer than he had left it. On his return he met with a wonderful adventure, which was to have some strange results.

Night had fallen as he was riding through a thick woods, and he lost his way, though he fancied he could not be far from home. His weary horse still carried him on, and he looked anxiously round for some building where he could find shelter until morning; for the rain was beating down and the wolves howled in the darkness round about.

All at once he became aware of a long avenue of trees, at the end of which a light glimmered. This proved to be a lamp, hung at the entrance to a large and splendid palace.

WELCOME, WEARY WAYFARER

was written in Eastern characters over the heavy, massive gate of iron. This gate appeared to be closed; but at the merchant's approach, to his great amazement, it swung slowly back on its hinges, though no porter appeared to open it. The message over the gate emboldened the wayfarer to ride into the courtyard; and an inner door, also opening of itself, disclosed a large stable, with every convenience for fifty horses, but quite empty.

The merchant put up his weary horse, fed him on the oats and hay he saw ready to hand, and then went to try and find someone in the palace. In the vestibule was a fountain which sent up a sparkling jet from a marble basin, and gave a delicious air of coolness to all around. From this he went on through many large apartments, all splendidly furnished, but with no one in them – not even a servant to take care of the house. In one of the rooms a fire was burning, and here was a table containing some very tempting dishes, though there was only one plate and a single knife and fork. After waiting in doubt for some time, hoping the owner of the house would appear, the hungry merchant sat down and had a hearty meal, drinking his own health afterwards.

As it was now time to rest, the merchant went upstairs. On the upper floor were several bedrooms, with large beds and handsome furniture. In one the merchant decided to pass the night, rightly thinking that the welcome to wayfarers inscribed over the gateway must include a bed upon which to repose. Still, he was puzzled that with all the order and neatness visible throughout the palace, no living being appeared to whom he could speak. But he was too tired to think very much about it, and soon fell fast asleep.

When he awoke the next morning, greatly refreshed, he was amazed to see that a new suit of clothes had been placed ready for him to put on instead of his own, which were torn and travelstained.

"Surely," he thought, "this place must belong to some kind fairy who has taken pity on my ill-luck."

He then went downstairs to the room where he had supped, and was pleased, though not altogether surprised, to find the breakfast-table ready prepared, with everything he could wish to eat and drink.

Seeing that a door leading to a beautiful garden stood open, he put on his hat, hoping that he might meet his kind host and have an opportunity of thanking him.

In the garden also everything was in first-rate order. The flower-beds were full of beautiful plants, the walks clean and hard, the grass-plots soft and smooth as velvet carpets.

At the end of one path stood a lovely stone seat, shaded by a splendid rose tree in full bloom. This set the merchant thinking of his daughter Beauty's wish for a red rose; he selected the very best he could find and plucked it. A moment later came a tremendous roar, like that of an angry lion disturbed by a hunter. In terror, he fell on his knees and covered his face with his hands, dreading to look up, lest he should see some wild beast ready to spring upon him. Then he heard another great roar, and a heavy hand was laid on his shoulder: he rose and saw a monster with a beast's head but of the shape of a man, covered with fur. The creature stood glaring at him in a threatening manner, and then said, in a terrible voice, "Ungrateful man! I saved your life by admitting you into my palace. I gave you rest and refreshment and clothes, and you reject my kindness by stealing the only thing I prize – my beautiful roses. For this you shall surely atone. Prepare for death!"

The merchant, in utter terror, again fell on his knees and begged for forgiveness, calling the Beast "my lord," and declaring that he meant no harm, but had only plucked the rose for his youngest daughter, whom he loved, and who wished for one.

"I will spare no one who steals my roses," roared the Beast, "whatever excuse he makes."

The merchant again pleaded for his life, telling how his daughter, Beauty, had asked for nothing but a single rose, while her sisters had desired jewels and beautiful clothes. At last he prevailed.

"You shall have your life on one condition," replied the Beast. "You have told me this story of your daughters, but how am I to know that it is true? I will spare your life and allow you to go home only if you promise to bring one of them to suffer in your stead. If she refuses to come, you must promise faithfully to be back yourself within three months. And don't call me 'my lord,' for I hate flattery; I am not a lord, but a Beast! Promise, or die! and choose quickly!"

The merchant, who was very tender-hearted, had not the least intention of letting one of his daughters die for his sake; but he thought it best to agree to the Beast's conditions, for he would at least have the satisfaction of seeing his family again. So he gave his promise and turned sorrowfully away.

"Go to the room you slept in," cried the Beast after him; "you may fill a chest with gold and jewels or whatsoever you like best to take home with you, but woe betide you if you are not back on the appointed day."

When he reached the room the merchant, reflecting that he must in any case die – for, being an upright and honest man, he had no thought of breaking a promise made even to a Beast – decided that he might as well have the comfort of leaving his children well provided for, especially as there were heaps of gold pieces lying about. He accordingly filled the chest with gold and departed, leaving the palace as sorrowful as he had been glad when he first beheld it.

When he reached his own house, his daughters warmly welcomed him, but were struck with the sadness settled in his face. In silence he gave the elder sisters the costly presents he had brought for them, and then sat down, evidently still very troubled. Beauty ran at once and threw her arms round his neck to comfort him.

Every evening at supper the Beast would ask, "Beauty, will
you marry me?"

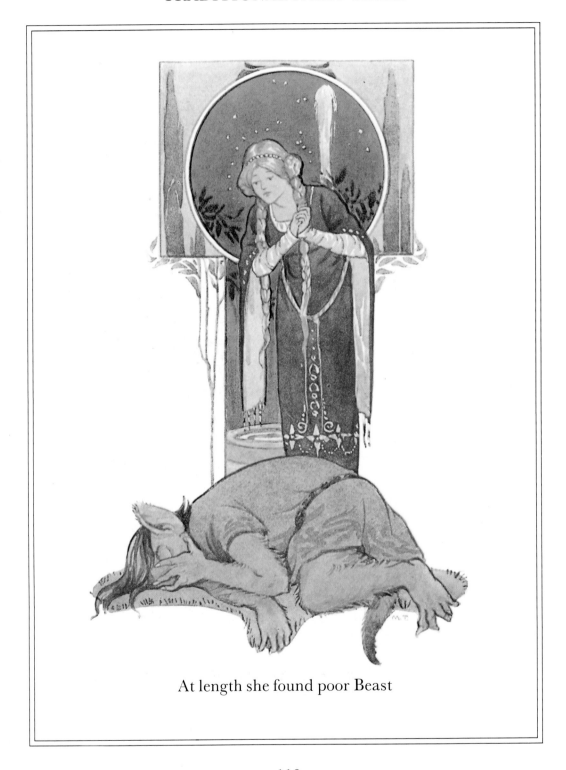

At length she found poor Beast

"Ah, my dear Beauty, here is your red rose," said the merchant; "but you little know the price your poor father has promised to pay for it." And he told her everything that had occurred.

The elder sisters stopped examining their presents and came up to listen. When they understood the cause of their father's sadness, they began to throw all the blame on poor Beauty. "If the affected little thing had only asked for presents like ours," they declared, "this trouble would not have come, and our dear father would not be in danger of his life. She pretends to be so much better than other people, but though she will be the cause of her father's death she does not shed a single tear."

"It would be quite useless to do so," said Beauty quietly, "for my father will not die. As the Beast said he would accept one of the daughters, I am going to give myself up to him, and so prove my love for the best of fathers."

The brothers would not hear of this and begged hard to be allowed to go and kill the monster. The father, however, was firm to his pledge, and knew that the Beast would not be put off. He also had secret hopes that Beauty's life would after all be spared; for the Beast's generosity had made him think that, as he had relented so far as to send him away with piles of gold, his intentions might not be so murderous as his words. He also hoped that the appearance of Beauty and her charming manners would produce an effect, as they had always done in her own home; and that the monster would not really care to take the life of so young and innocent a creature.

The sisters secretly exulted at Beauty's sad fate, for they had always been jealous of her, because she was loved the most by their father. But the brothers were really and truly grieved, and kissed their sister heartily when the three months had expired and the time had come for her to set out with her father on their sorrowful journey.

The domain around the Beast's castle was very beautiful. Birds with splendid plumage flew about, singing merry songs as they built their nests in the thick trees. In spite of the sorrowful nature of their errand, Beauty and her father could not help feeling a little comforted by the beauty of the scene; and the nearer they came to the Beast's palace, the fresher became the grass, and the thicker the throng of chirping birds.

In due time they reached the palace, which they found deserted, as on the merchant's first visit. The horse, without bidding, went into the same stable as before. In the spacious reception-hall they found a magnificent supper laid, with covers for two persons. There was every imaginable dainty on the table, but Beauty could hardly eat a bite for terror, while her father was overwhelmed with fear of what was to come. He had seen the terrible Beast, and knew what a large mouth and ugly fangs he had, and how, in every respect, he was just the sort of creature to frighten Beauty out of her wits, and he dreaded what might be the effect of the Beast's appearance.

When supper was over, a heavy tread sounded along the corridor; the door of the room was thrown open, and the Beast stalked in. And, oh, he was far, far uglier than Beauty imagined he possibly could be! And he had *such* a mouth, and two such ugly teeth came right over his lower jaw!

Beauty did her best to hide her fear. The creature walked right up to her, eyed her all over, and then asked in a gruff voice:

"Have you come here of your own free will?"

"Yes," she faltered.

The monster then said in a softened tone, "You are a good girl. I am much obliged to you."

This mild manner somewhat raised the hopes of the merchant; but they were instantly damped by the Beast's turning towards him, and gruffly commanding him to quit the castle and never return again under pain of death. Having given this order in a tone which showed he intended to be obeyed, the Beast retired with a bow and a goodnight to Beauty, and a glance at her father which seemed to say, "Make haste."

"Ah, my dear Beauty," said the merchant, kissing his daughter tenderly, "I am half dead already at the thought of leaving you at the mercy of this dreadful Beast. You shall go back home and leave me here."

"No, indeed," said Beauty boldly, "I will never agree to that. You must go at once, or the Beast will certainly kill you."

At length the merchant departed, after kissing his daughter again a score of times, while she, poor girl, tried to raise his spirits by feigning a courage she was far from feeling. When he had gone, she took a lighted candle and wandered along the corridor in search of her room: soon she came to a door on which was inscribed in large letters:

BEAUTY'S ROOM

She timidly opened the door and found herself in a large room, beautifully furnished, with bookcases, sofas, pictures, and a guitar and other musical instruments to help her while away the time.

"The Beast does not mean to eat me up at once," she thought, "or he would never have taken all this trouble."

So, a little comforted, she retired to rest, and, exhausted with her journey and her fears, quickly fell asleep.

Next morning she examined her room more closely. On the first leaf of an album was written her own name – Beauty – and beneath it, in letters of gold, she read the following verse:–

"Beauteous lady, dry your tears;
Here's no cause for sighs or fears:
Command as freely as you may,
For you command and I obey."

This was a very comforting verse indeed, but Beauty still felt very unhappy, very lonely, and very anxious to know what was to befall her.

"Ah!" sighed the poor girl, "if I might have a wish granted, it would be to see my poor father and what he is doing."

She turned as she spoke and, to her great surprise, saw in a mirror opposite a picture of her home. The merchant, distracted with grief, was lying on a couch; and her two sisters were at the window, looking listlessly out. At this sight poor Beauty wept bitterly; but after a time she regained her fortitude, and went down to the dining-hall. She wondered not a little to see the hall still quite empty. Not a person appeared to welcome her, but a dainty meal had been spread, as on the previous day. But at supper, as she was about to seat herself at table, the Beast came in and humbly requested permission to stay and see her eat.

Beauty, who somehow did not feel nearly so much afraid of him and was utterly tired of being alone, replied, "Yes, if you wish to do so."

All the while she was eating the Beast sat by, looking at her very respectfully but with great admiration. He soon began to talk, and astonished her by his wit and the extent of his knowledge on various subjects. At last he leaned over the table and, peering intently at her face, asked suddenly:

"Do you think me so very, very ugly?"

Beauty was obliged to reply, "Yes, shockingly ugly!" but, fearing to hurt his feelings, added that he could not help his looks.

This did not seem to console the poor Beast much, for he sighed deeply. After sitting a while in silence, he seemed to collect all his courage for one grand effort and asked Beauty – to her great astonishment – "Will you marry me?"

"No, Beast," she replied at once in a very decided way; whereupon her suitor gave a great sigh which nearly blew out the candles, and retired, looking very doleful.

For some little time Beauty's life was a very quiet one. She roamed about the palace and through the gardens just as she pleased, invisible attendants bringing her whatever she wished for. Each evening the Beast would come to supper, and try to entertain her as best he could. He was so well-informed and talked so sensibly that Beauty began to like him. Still, his hideous form shocked her each time she looked at him; and whenever her host, after doing his utmost to be agreeable all the evening, repeated his question, "Will you marry me, Beauty?" she always gave a very decided refusal in the unmistakable words, "No, Beast."

Then the Beast would give one of his tremendous sighs and retire; but the next evening he was always there again, and when he asked the old question, "Beauty, will you marry me?" she always replied, "No, Beast."

But soon Beauty began to be homesick; the more so, as her magic mirror, which she never failed to consult each day, showed that her father was pining for her very much. His sons had gone to fight their country's battles, and his two eldest daughters had got married and were constantly fighting with their husbands. So, you see, the merchant was rather sad and lonely.

At last Beauty summoned up courage to beg the Beast to let her go home and see her father. He was at first much alarmed at the proposal, fearing she might forget to come back again; but at last he consented, after exacting a promise that she would not be away long.

He spoke very kindly to her on the matter, and indeed always treated her with great kindness and courtesy, though she had so frequently refused to marry him.

"Tomorrow morning," said the Beast, "you will find yourself at your father's house. But pray, pray do not forget me in my loneliness. When you are ready to come back, you have only to lay the ring I now give you on your dressing-table before you lie down at night."

Beauty took the ring, and the Beast bade her a sorrowful farewell.

Beauty retired to rest; and, sure enough, when she awoke in the morning, she was in her old bed at her father's house. By the glimmering light of dawn, she could see that nothing in the room had changed. It was all kept, by her father's directions, just as she had left it. But one thing surprised and pleased her greatly, for which she could not in any way account. By the bedside lay a large chest full of beautiful apparel and costly jewels.

You may fancy how glad her father was to see her. But the envious sisters, who were there on a visit, were not at all pleased. When they saw the chest they at once declared that the presents must have been intended by the Beast for them; whereupon the box disappeared to show that they were mistaken.

On the failure of this selfish scheme, they resolved, as they termed it, "to serve her out" by making her stay too long, hoping the Beast would be very angry, and punish her accordingly. The days passed happily away; and the sisters behaved with such false kindness that Beauty was prevailed upon to stay. So the days glided by, and Beauty prolonged her visit, first for one week, and then two weeks, longer than she had intended to stay.

But what was the Beast doing all this while? He was very, very lonely in his palace, vainly waiting the return of his beloved Beauty. Every evening, at sunset, he would lie on the grass in his garden, thinking of her till his very heart ached with longing.

One evening, as Beauty sat with her father at their evening meal, a likeness of the Beast suddenly appeared before her, like a figure in a magic lantern. He was very pale, and looked dreadfully thin and woeful. Directly Beauty saw the vision she was touched with remorse and regretted that she had broken her word. The mournful eyes of the poor Beast, as they turned towards her, seemed to wear a look of reproach, and she remembered how kindly he had always treated her and what pains he had taken to gratify her slightest wish. This cut her to the heart; and, that night, without saying a word to anyone, she laid the ring on the table when she went to bed.

When she awoke she was again in the Beast's palace; but no Beast appeared to welcome her. She had dressed herself very carefully, hoping to please him, but hour after hour went by and he did not appear, until at last she became dreadfully alarmed. She ran into the courtyard thinking he might be there awaiting her coming; but he was not to be seen. Then she hurried up the great staircase, and looked into room after room; all were empty and silent, and the longer she searched the more she sorrowed, for the thought came to her that perhaps the poor Beast was dead.

Then she went into the garden, calling his name, and at length found poor Beast stretched out on the grass-plot close to the fountain, to all appearance dead. His eyes were closed, and he did not seem even to breathe.

Beauty had never known till now how fond she was of the Beast, and the prospect of losing him altogether was more than she could bear. She tried every effort to bring him back to life, kneeling beside him, and moistening his temples with water. Then she called him every endearing name she could think of, and at last, in very despair, brought a large bowl of water and emptied it over his prostrate form. At this the Beast opened his eyes, a gleam of joy shot across his face, and he gasped:

"Have you come back at last, Beauty? I have waited long for you and despaired of ever seeing you again. But now I have looked on you once more, I can die quite happily."

"No! no!" cried Beauty; "my own dear Beast, you must not die. You have been very kind to me – much kinder than I deserve – and you are so good that I do not mind your looks; and indeed – indeed – I – I would be your wife if you were twenty times as ugly!"

And she flung her arms round the Beast's neck, and kissed his great hairy cheek.

At this a great crash was heard. The palace was suddenly lit up from basement to roof, hundreds of most glorious lamps – blue, and yellow, and green, and red – gleaming like wondrous jewels. Then came a burst of music, delicious voices and instruments in harmony, and the whole scene was one of rejoicing and festivity. For a moment Beauty stood bewildered at the sudden change of scene; then a gentle, grateful pressure of her hand recalled her to herself, and she beheld, with astonishment, that the Beast had been transformed into a graceful and handsome young Prince.

"But where is Beast? I do not know you. I want my Beast, my lovely Beast!" exclaimed Beauty.

The Prince answered her with eyes beaming.

"I am he, dear Beauty. A wicked fairy had laid me under a spell, and transformed me into the shape of a hideous beast, which I was to retain until a beautiful girl should consent, of her own free will, to marry me. You have done so: your goodness of heart and your gratitude made you overlook my ugliness; and in consenting to become the wife of the Beast you have restored me to happiness."

Beauty, still greatly surprised, but radiant with happiness, let the Prince lead her back to his palace and summon her father for their wedding.

TOM THUMB

ong, long ago, in the days of good King Arthur, there lived a very wonderful magician and enchanter, known as Merlin.

One day, while on a long journey, feeling hungry and tired, he looked round for a place in which to get rest and refreshment, and soon caught sight of a workman's cottage.

Merlin walked in; and whether it was his long beard that inspired respect, or whether it was that the people of the house were nice kindly folks, it is certain that the enchanter could not have been better received had he been King Arthur himself. The best bread and a bowl of fresh milk were placed before him, and the good woman, in particular, seemed most anxious to please her guest.

Merlin, however, saw that something was troubling his hosts, and as he rested he tried to find out the cause of their grief. The wife would not reply; but the husband, after scratching his head a long while without finding any ideas, answered "that they were sorry because they had no children."

"If we only had a son, sir," he went on, "even a very little one, no bigger than my thumb, we should be as happy as the days are long."

Merlin was very fond of a joke, and the idea of this great strapping ploughman having a son no bigger than his thumb amused him intensely.

"You shall have your wish, my friend," said the magician with a smile; and after bidding them farewell he went away.

You may fancy that a man like Merlin had many friends among the fairies. Even Oberon, the Fairy King, knew him and loved him. What was of more importance in this case, Merlin was more friendly with the Queen of the Fairies. Immediately on his return from his journey he went to her and told of his visit to the cottage and of the ploughman's strange request. Both agreed that it would be a fine joke to let the good man have exactly what he had asked for, neither more nor less.

Not a great while afterwards the ploughman's wife had a son; but you can imagine the worthy man's surprise when he first saw him, for the baby was exactly the size he had asked for – as big as his thumb! In every respect it was the prettiest little doll baby you could wish to see. The Queen of the Fairies herself came in soon after it was born, and summoned the most skillful of her followers to clothe the little stranger as a fairy child should be clothed. A fairy verse tells us:

> *An acorn that he had for his crown,*
> *His shirt it was by spiders spun;*
> *His coat was woven of thistle-down,*
> *His trousers up with tags were done;*
> *His stockings, of apple-rind, they tie*
> *With eye-lash plucked from his mother's eye;*
> *His shoes were made of a mouse's skin,*
> *Nicely tanned, with the hair within.*

Strange to say, Tom, although he grew older, as everybody has to, never grew bigger; so that the ploughman often wished he had merely asked for a son without saying anything about the young gentleman's size. And he agreed with his wife in wishing he had not mentioned his thumb, or that Merlin had not granted his wish so exactly to the letter; for he feared such a little fellow would never be able to defend himself against the rude boys of the village. But the ploughman need have had no fears, for what Tom lacked in size he made up for in cunning, and this made him a match for any urchin in the place.

For instance, when he played at "cherry-stones" with the village boys and lost all his stones he would creep into the bags of all the winners, and steal his losings back again. The boys could not first understand how it was that Tom Thumb always won, but at last he was caught in the act, and the owner of the bag, an ugly, ill-natured boy, cried out, "Ah, Master Tom Thumb! I've caught you at last and now won't I reward you for thieving!" Then he pulled the strings of the bag so tightly round Tom's neck as almost to strangle him, and gave the bag shake after shake, which knocked all the cherry-stones against Tom's legs like so many pebbles, and bruised him sadly. At last Tom was allowed to come out and run home, rubbing his shins ruefully, and promising he would "play fair" next time. But the boys saved him all trouble in the matter by refusing to play with him at all.

The next scrape Tom got into was a rather serious one. One day his mother was making a batter pudding. Tom, like a good many children, was rather fond of putting his nose into what did not concern him, and he climbed to the edge of the bowl to see if his mother mixed it properly, and to remind her, if necessary, about such little matters as putting plenty of sugar in. As he sat on the edge of the bowl his foot

The cook carried Tom on a platter to the King

The Queen of the Fairies sent him flying once more
to the Court

slipped and he went into the batter head over heels; in fact, plunged into it as boys splash into a swimming pool. The batter got into his mouth so that he could not cry out; and he kicked and struggled so that he was soon covered with batter and quite disappeared in the thick, sticky pudding.

His mother chanced to be looking away at the time, and did not see what happened. Then the pudding was tied up in a cloth and popped into the pot to boil. The water soon grew hot, and poor Tom began to kick and plunge with all his might. His mother, who had stirred him around and around, thinking that he was something in the nature of a lump of suet (for Tom, being covered with batter, could not be seen), wondered what caused the pudding to keep bumping against the top and sides of the pot. She took off the lid to see. She was surprised to see the pudding bobbing up and down in the pot, dancing a sort of hornpipe all by itself. She could scarcely believe her eyes, and was very much frightened. At last, deciding that the pudding must be bewitched, she determined to give it to the first person who came by.

She had not long to wait before a wandering tinker passed, crying, "Pots and kettles to mend, oh! – pots and kettles to mend, oh!"

Tom's mother beckoned him in and gave him the pudding. The tinker, delighted to have so fine a pudding for his dinner, thanked the good woman, put it in his pouch, and trudged merrily on. But he had not gone far before he felt a funny sort of "bump – bump – bump!" in his pouch. At first he thought a rat had somehow got in, and opened the bag to see; but, to his horror, he heard a voice from inside the pudding calling, "Hullo! hullo! hul-l-l-o-o!" There was the pudding moving in his bag, and two little feet sticking out of it, wriggling in the funniest way possible.

At this the tinker stared till his eyes almost started from his head, for he had never seen a pudding with feet before. The voice cried, "Let me ou-u-ut! Let me ou-u-ut!" and the pudding kicked and danced in the most alarming manner.

The tinker, who was very frightened, at once granted the request made, as he thought, by the pudding. He not only "let" it out but "flung" it out, right over the hedge. Then he took to his heels, and ran as hard as he could for more than a mile without once stopping to look behind. As for the pudding, it fell into a dry ditch with a great splodge, breaking into five or six pieces. Tom crept out, battered all over and battered inside.

He managed, however, to get home, crawling along like a fly that has been rescued from a cream jug. His mother was only too glad to see him. With much difficulty she washed the batter off and put him to bed.

Another day Tom went with his mother to milk the cow. As it was rather windy, his mother wisely tied her little son to a thistle with a needleful of thread, in case he was blown away. But the cow, while chewing the thistles, happened to choose the very one to which tiny Tom was tied, and gulped thistle and boy in a single mouthful. Tom, finding himself in a large red cavern, with two rows of great white "grinders" going "champ – champ!" cried out with fright, "Mother! Mother!"

"Where are you, Tommy, my dear?" cried the good woman in alarm.

"Here, mother!" screamed Tom; "in the brown cow's mouth!"

The mother began to weep and wring her hands, for she thought her dear little boy would be crushed into a shapeless mass. The cow, surprised at such strange noises in her throat, opened her mouth wide and dropped Tommy on the grass. His mother was only too glad to wrap him up in her apron and run home with him.

Tom was rather forward for his age, and still more so for size, and he soon thought he ought in some way to make himself useful. To indulge the little man, his father made him a whip of a barley straw to drive the plough horses. Tom thought this very grand, and used to shout at the horses and crack his whip in fine style; but as he could never strike a horse higher than the hoof, it is doubtful whether he was of much use.

One day, as he stood on a stone to aim a blow at one of the horses, his foot slipped, and he rolled over and over into a deep furrow. A raven hovering nearby picked up the barley-straw whip and little Tommy at one gulp. Up through the air the little man was whisked, so swiftly that it took his breath away. Presently the raven stopped to rest on the terrace of a castle belonging to a giant called Grumbo. Here the raven dropped Tom, and old Grumbo, coming out on the terrace for a walk, spied him perched upon a stone. Without thinking, the cruel monster snapped him up and swallowed him, clothes and all, as if he had been a pill. But Grumbo would have been wiser had he left Tom alone; for the little boy at once began to jump and dance in such a way as to make the greedy giant very uncomfortable in his stomach.

Grumbo kicked and roared, and rubbed himself to

relieve the pain; but the more he rubbed, the more Tom danced, until at last the giant became dreadfully unwell. He opened his mouth, and his inside feelings seemed to grow worse and worse, until suddenly the little passenger came flying out, right over the terrace, into the sea.

A big fish happened to be swimming by at the time, and seeing little Tom whirling through the air, took him for a kind of May fly. So he opened his mouth and swallowed. Poor Tom was now in worse plight than ever; for if he made the fish set him free, as he had made the giant, he would only have been dropped in the sea and been drowned. His only chance now was to wait patiently in the hope that the fish would be caught. It was not long before this happened; for the fish was a greedy fellow, always in search of something to eat, and never satisfied. He snapped up a bait hanging at the end of a fishing-line, and in another instant was wriggling and writhing with the hook through his gills. He was dragged up, and the fisherman, seeing what a splendid fellow he was, thought he would present him to King Arthur. So, having killed his prize, the fisherman made his way to Court, where he received a warm welcome in the royal kitchen.

The fish was much admired, and the cook took a

knife and proceeded to cut it open. What a surprise he got when Master Tom popped up his head, and politely hoped that cook was "quite well!"

You can understand the amazement this unexpected arrival caused. King Arthur was quickly informed that a wee knight, of extraordinary height, had come to Court, and Master Tom met a very hearty reception. The King made him his dwarf, and he soon became loved by the whole Court as the funniest, merriest little fellow they had ever seen.

In dancing Tom greatly excelled; and it became a custom with the King to place him on the table for the diversion of the company. But Tom could also run and jump with wonderful agility, and was sometimes known to leap over a thread stretched across the table at a height of 3½ inches. Once he tried to leap over a reel of cotton that was too high for him, and he fell over and hurt himself.

He had at least as much cleverness in his head as in his heels, if not more. The Queen soon grew very fond of him; and as for King Arthur he scarcely ever went hunting without having Tom Thumb riding astride on his saddle-bow. If it began to rain, the little man would creep into the King's pocket, and lie there snug and warm until the shower was over; and sometimes the King would set him to ride upon his thumb, with a piece of silk cord passed through a ring for a bridle, and a whip made of a tiny stalk of grass.

One day King Arthur questioned Tom about his parentage and birth, for he was naturally curious to know where his clever little page came from.

Tom replied that his parents were poor people, and that he would be very glad of an opportunity to see them. To this the King freely consented; and so that he should not go empty-handed, gave him an order on the royal treasury for as much money as he could carry. Tom made choice of a silver three-penny piece, and, having procured a little purse, with much difficulty tied it on his back. His burden made his progress very slow and hard, but he managed at last to reach home safely, having travelled half a mile in forty-eight hours.

There was great rejoicing on the part of his parents, for they had feared he was dead. They were especially surprised at the large sum of money he had brought. A walnut shell was placed for him by the fire-side, and his parents feasted him on a hazel-nut. But they were not as careful as they should have been, for they allowed him to eat the whole nut in three days, whereas a nut generally lasted him for a month. The consequence was that Tommy was ill and had to lie three days in the walnut shell.

When he got well he thought it time to return to his duties at the palace; and his mother, though sorry to part with him, took him in her hand, and with one puff blew him all the way to King Arthur's Court.

Here a sad disaster was in store for Tom – greater than any he had yet met. His mother had hoped he would have the good fortune that had always attended him; for indeed little Tom Thumb had gone through dangers enough to have killed three ordinary men. If she had thought of this danger she would doubtless have taken him back herself; but she trusted to chance. And, indeed, if the wind had been a little stronger, or a little steadier, he would have alighted quite safely. Instead of doing so, however, the little man came down – splash! – into a bowl of furmenty, a kind of soup of which the King was very fond, and which the royal cook was then carrying across the courtyard for the King's special enjoyment.

The splash sent the hot furmenty into the cook's eyes, and he dropped the bowl.

"Oh dear! oh dear!" he cried as he watched the rich liquor run away and thought how angry and disappointed the King would be.

Then, to save his own skin, the artful cook pretended that Tom had played the trick on purpose to be disrespectful to His Majesty. So poor Tom was placed on his trial for high treason, found guilty, and sentenced to be beheaded.

Alarmed at the cruel sentence, he looked round for a way to escape. He saw a miller listening to the proceedings, with his mouth wide open like a great cavern. Tom, with a sudden bound, sprang down the miller's throat, unseen by all, and unknown even to the miller himself.

The prisoner having escaped, the court broke up, and the miller, who had got a touch of the hiccups, hurried home. Now Tom, having escaped from his stern judges, was equally desirous to do so from the miller's interior, which reminded him of the days when he had been swallowed by the brown cow. So, thinking the miller ought to know what was in his inside, Tom danced so many jigs and cut so many capers that the poor man, in a state of great alarm, sent messengers in every direction for medical aid.

He soon had the satisfaction of being surrounded by five learned men, among whom a fierce dispute arose as to the nature of his illness. One said that watching the mill sails turn had made him giddy; a second said this could hardly be, for the miller was used to seeing them turn. The third declared the patient must have swallowed some water by mistake, for he certainly was not used to that, and it had disagreed. The dispute lasted so long that the miller, growing tired, gave a great yawn. Tom saw his chance and sprang out, alighting on his feet in the middle of the table. The miller, seeing who the little creature was, and remembering how he had tormented him, flew into a great rage and flung Tom out of the open window into the river.

A large salmon happened to be passing and snapped him up in a moment. Soon afterwards the salmon was caught and placed in the market-place for sale. It was bought by the steward of a great lord; but this nobleman, thinking it a right royal fish, did not eat it himself, but sent it to King Arthur as a present. The cross old cook had the fish given to him to prepare for dinner; and when he came to cut it open, out jumped his old acquaintance, Tom Thumb. The cook was glad to be able to wreak his spite once more on his old enemy; and indeed Tom had played him too many tricks in his time, never thinking the day would come when it would be the cook's turn to play the tricks and Tommy's turn to bear them.

The cook determined to have vengeance, so he seized poor Tom and carried him on a platter to the King, expecting that Arthur would order the culprit to be executed. But the King had no such idea, and besides, he was fully occupied with affairs of State, so he ordered the cook to bring Tom another day. The cook, although obliged to obey, was determined to serve Tom out while he could; so he shut him up in a mouse-trap for a whole week – and very miserable Tom felt. By the end of the week the King's anger was gone. He freely forgave Tom and ordered him a new suit of clothes and a good-sized mouse to ride on for a horse. Some time after he was even admitted to the order of knighthood, and became known in the land as Sir Thomas Thumb.

An old song tells what a very fine little knight he was:

> *"His shirt was made of butterflies' wings,*
> *His boots were made of chicken skins,*
> *His coat and breeches were made with pride,*
> *A tailor's needle hung by his side,*
> *A mouse for a horse he used to ride."*

The mouse-steed was a very pretty present, and little Tom rode on it, morning, noon, and night, until at last it was the means of bringing him into very great danger.

One day, when Tom was riding by a farmhouse, a

large cat, seeing the mouse, rushed upon it. Tom, drawing his sword, defended himself in the bravest manner possible, and managed to keep the cat at bay until King Arthur and his knights came up. But little Sir Thomas had not passed through the combat unhurt – some of his wounds were deep and dangerous.

They took him home and laid him on a bed of down on an ivory couch; but still, with all possible care and kindness, he grew worse, and it seemed that he would die. But then his old friend, the Queen of the Fairies, appeared and bore him away to Fairy-land, where she kept him for several years. Then, dressing him in bright green, she climbed an almond tree covered with blossom and sent him flying once more to the Court.

But by this time King Arthur, who had missed his little friend sadly and had often wished to have him back, was no longer there to welcome him. There had been great changes while little Sir Thomas Thumb had lived among the fairies, joining in their sports by night, and helping to make fairy rings. Good King Arthur was dead, and King Thunstone sat on the throne instead.

The people flocked together from far and near to see the wonderful little hero. King Thunstone asked who he was, where he lived, and whence he came; and the little man replied:

> *"My name is Tom Thumb,*
> *From the Fairies I come.*
> *When King Arthur shone,*
> *This court was my home.*
> *In me he delighted,*
> *By him I was knighted.*
> *Did you never hear of*
> *Sir Thomas Thumb?"*

The King and his courtiers all smiled at the little fellow's fine verses, and the King ordered a tiny chair to be made, in order that Tom might sit on the royal table. He also caused a little palace of gold, a span high, to be built, for Tom to live in. The door was just an inch wide. Last of all, he gave him a lovely little coach to ride in, drawn by six small mice. The Queen was a rather silly woman, and because the King did not give her a new coach too, she became very jealous of Tom and told the King that he had insulted her.

The King sent for him in a great rage, and to escape his fury our hero had to fly from the Court. An empty snail-shell afforded him a secure retreat for a long time, and he did not venture out till he was nearly starved.

At last the tiny fellow saw a butterfly approach his hiding-place. He sprang on its back, and it flew from flower to flower, from field to field, till at last it brought him back to King Thunstone's Court. The King, the Queen, the knights, and the cook all tried to catch the butterfly, but could not. At last poor Tom, having neither saddle or bridle, slipped from his seat and fell into a watercan, where he was nearly drowned.

The Queen vowed he should still be beheaded, and he was put back into the mouse-trap. But that night, a cat, seeing something move and supposing it to be a mouse, patted the trap about until she broke it, and Tom was able to make another dash for freedom.

The Queen, thinking that he bore a charmed life, and must therefore be a special friend of the fairies, at last forgave him, and he was reinstated in royal esteem. After that he lived for several years, having many more wonderful adventures and fights with animals of various kinds.

HANSEL AND GRETEL

ear a large wood once lived a poor wood-cutter with his wife and two children. The little boy was called Hansel and the little girl Gretel. They rarely had nice things to eat, and when there was a famine in the land they could not get so much as their daily bread. As he lay in bed at night their father was greatly troubled; he sighed and groaned and said to his wife:

"What is to become of us? How are we to feed our little ones when we haven't anything ourselves?"

"I tell you what, husband," answered the woman, "tomorrow morning early we will lead the children far into the woods, light them a fire, give each a bit of bread, and then go to our work and leave them alone. They will never find their way home, and we shall be rid of them."

"No, wife," said the man, "I cannot do that; how could anyone have the heart to leave two dear children alone in the wood to be devoured by wild beasts?"

"Oh!" said she, "then we must all four die of hunger." But she continued to persuade him, and at last he half consented.

The two children were so hungry that they had not been able to go to sleep, and they had overheard what their step-mother proposed to do with them. Gretel wept bitter tears and said to Hansel, "It is all up with us."

"Don't cry, Gretel," said Hansel, "I will see that this does not happen."

When the old couple had fallen asleep, he put on his little coat, crept downstairs, and let himself out the back door. The moon was shining brightly, and the white pebbles on the path in front of the house shone like new coins. Hansel stooped and stuffed his coat pockets full of pebbles. Then he went back and said to Gretel, "Be comforted, little sister, and go to sleep. God will not forsake us;" and he lay down on his little bed.

When day dawned the woman called the two children and told them to dress before the sun was high. "Get up, both of you," she said, "and come into the woods and pick up sticks." Then she gave each a piece of bread, and told them to keep it for dinner and not eat it before, as they would get nothing else. Gretel put the bread under her apron, because

Gretel had taken out a window pane and sat down to enjoy it

The King rode with Gretel to his palace, the fawn running
along behind them

Hansel's pockets were full of pebbles.

Soon after, they all started together for the woods. They had not gone far before Hansel stood still and looked back at the house. He did this again and again, till his father said, "Hansel, what are you gaping at?"

"Oh, father," said Hansel, "I am looking at my white kitten, who is sitting on the roof waving me goodbye."

"That isn't your kitten, silly child," said the woman, "it's the morning sunlight shining on the chimney." But Hansel had not really been looking at the kitten; he was scattering behind him the pebbles out of his pocket.

When they came to the middle of the woods the father said, "Now, children, pick up sticks, and we will make a fire."

Hansel and Gretel built up quite a pile of twigs, and when the fire was alight and the flames were rising high, the woman said, "You can lie down by the fire and rest yourselves while we go further to chop wood. When we have finished we will come and fetch you."

Hansel and Gretel sat by the fire, and when dinner-time came ate their bread, and because they heard the blows of the hatchet they thought their father was not far off. But it was not the hatchet they heard, but a branch that he had tied to a rotten tree, and which the wind blew up and down. They sat such a long time that for very weariness they closed their eyes and went to sleep. They did not wake till it was night and pitch dark. Gretel began to cry and said, "We shall never find our way out of the woods."

"Wait," said Hansel, "the moon will be up soon, and then we'll find our way fast enough."

Before long the great full moon rose in the sky, and Hansel took his little sister's hand and followed the track of the pebbles, which shone like new silver coins and showed them the way. They walked the whole night, and at break of day reached their father's house. They knocked at the door, and when the woman opened it and saw Hansel and Gretel she said, "Why did you sleep so long in the woods? We began to think you were not coming back at all."

The father was delighted to see the children, for it had gone to his heart to leave them so cruelly.

Not long afterwards there was again great distress, and the children heard their stepmother saying to their father in the night, "There is hardly anything left to eat, only half a loaf of bread, and when that is gone what are we to do? The children must be done away with. We will take them deeper into the woods this time, so they will not be able to find their way out. It's the only thing to be done to save us."

The man's heart was heavy, and he thought to himself, "I would rather share our last crust with the children." But the woman had made up her mind, and all the man said made no difference. When you have said "A" you must say "B" too, and as he had given in the first time he was obliged to give in the second time.

The wakeful children, however, had heard the whole of the conversation. When his parents had gone to sleep, Hansel got up again to go out as he had done before and pick up pebbles, but he found that the woman had locked the door. All the same, he comforted his little sister, saying, "Never mind, Gretel, don't cry, but go to sleep. God will take care of us."

At dawn the woman came and roused the children. She gave them each a slice of bread, but it was smaller than last time.

As they walked to the woods Hansel crumbled the bread in his pocket, stood still now and then, and dropped a crumb on the ground.

"Hansel, why do you loiter behind and look around?" his father asked.

"I am looking at my little dove, who it sitting on

the roof to coo goodbye."

"Stupid," cried the woman, "it is not your dove but the morning sun shining on the chimney." But Hansel went on dropping his crumbs by the way.

The woman led the children deeper and deeper into the woods, to a part where they had never been before. Again a huge fire was kindled, and the mother said, "Stay here, children, and when you are tired take a nap. We are going further to chop wood. When we have finished we will fetch you."

When dinner-time came Gretel divided her bread with Hansel, because he had scattered his as they came along. Then they fell asleep, and the evening went by without anyone coming to them. They did not wake till it was pitch dark. Hansel comforted his sister by saying, "Wait till the moon is up, then we shall see the bread crumbs I dropped on the ground, and that will show us the way home."

But when the moon rose they could see no bread crumbs, for the birds which flew in the woods and fields had picked up every one.

Hansel said, "We shall soon find our way, Gretel."

But they did not find it – though they walked the whole night and the whole of the next day, they were still in the woods and faint from hunger, for they had eaten nothing but a few berries. And now, because they were so tired and their legs would not carry them farther, they lay down under a tree and fell asleep.

The third morning after they had left their father's house they were still deeper in the woods and quite lost. If help did not come, they knew they would perish. Then they saw a beautiful snow-white bird sitting on a branch, and it was singing so beautifully that they stopped to listen. It spread its wings when it had finished its song, and flew in front of them, and they followed till it perched on the roof of a little house which, on coming near, they found was built of bread and thatched with cake, the windows being made of barley-sugar.

"We will set to work," said Hansel, "and made a good meal for once. I will have a good slice of the roof, and you, Gretel, shall begin with a window, which will taste nice and sweet."

Hansel climbed up and broke off a bit of the roof to see how it tasted, and Gretel stood by a window and nibbled it. Then, as they were happily eating, a voice called from inside –

"Nibble! nibble! nibble!
Who's nibbling at my house?"

The children answered –

> *"The wind, the wind,*
> *The child of heaven,"*

and went on eating, quite unconcerned.

Hansel, who found that the roof tasted very good, had torn off another great bit, and Gretel had taken out a window-pane and sat down to enjoy it. Suddenly the door opened and an old woman hobbled out. Hansel and Gretel shook in their shoes for fright, letting the good stuff fall from their hands.

The old woman nodded her old head and said, "Dear children, who brought you here? Come in do, and stay with me; no harm shall come to you!"

She took them by the hand and led them into the house. There a good dinner stood ready, milk pancakes, with sugar, apples, and nuts. Afterward, two little white beds were uncovered, and Hansel and Gretel lay down in them, feeling as if they were in heaven.

But the old woman was only pretending to be friendly; she was really a wicked old witch, who lay in wait for children, and had only had her house built of good things to eat in order to lure them into her clutches. When she had little ones safe in her power, she slaughtered, cooked, and ate them. The witch had pink eyes and could not see far, but she had a keen scent, like animals, and could smell human flesh a long way off. Directly Hansel and Gretel came near her house, she had laughed, chuckled wickedly and said to herself, "I'll have them on toast – they shan't escape."

Early the next morning, before the children were awake, she got up, and as she saw their round rosy cheeks, she muttered, "There's a tasty dish." Then she shook Hansel and, seizing him with her wrinkled hand, carried him to a little stable, where she shut him in behind a grating. He howled as loudly as he could, but it was no use. Next she went to Gretel, shook her and screamed, "Get up, lazy girl, and go and draw water to cook your brother something good, he is outside in the stable and must be fattened up; when he is fat I shall eat him."

Gretel began to cry bitterly, but she was forced to do what the wicked witch commanded.

Hansel was now given the most nourishing food, but Gretel got only crab-shells. Every morning the old witch hobbled to the stable and cried:

"Hansel, put your finger out that I may feel how fat you are getting." But Hansel used to stick out a bone instead of a finger, and the old woman, whose eyes were so dim that she could not see, marvelled that he did not grow fat.

When four weeks had passed, and Hansel still remained thin, she lost patience and declared she would not wait longer.

"Here, Gretel," she cried to the girl, "make haste and draw water – whether Hansel is fat or thin, I will kill and eat him tomorrow!"

The poor little sister wept and lamented as she brought the water, and tears poured down her cheeks! "Dear God, help us!" she prayed. "If the wild beasts had eaten us in the woods we should at least have died together."

When the witch had gone poor Gretel watched her chance and ran to Hansel, telling him what she had heard:

"We must run away quickly, for the old woman is a wicked witch, who will kill us."

But Hansel said: "I know how to get out, for I have loosened the fastening. But you must first steal her fairy wand, that we may save ourselves if she should follow, and bring, too, the pipe that hangs in her room."

Gretel managed to get both the wand and the pipe, and away the children went.

When the old witch came to see whether her meal

was ready, she sprang in a great rage to the window, and, though her eyes were bad, she spied the children running away.

She quickly put on her boots, which went yards at a step, and had scarcely made two steps with them before she overtook the children. But Gretel had seen that she was coming after them, and, by the help of the magic wand, turned Hansel into a lake of water, and herself into a swan which swam in the middle of it. The witch sat on the shore and tried to decoy the swan by throwing crumbs of bread to it; but it would not come near her, and she was at last forced to go home without her prisoners.

Then Gretel, by means of the wand, changed herself and Hansel back to their proper forms, and they journeyed on until dawn of day. The girl then turned herself into a beautiful rose in the midst of a thorny hedge; and Hansel sat by the side with his pipe.

Soon the witch came striding along.

"Good piper," she said, "may I pluck that beautiful rose?"

"Oh yes," said he.

She went to the hedge in a hurry to gather the flower – well knowing what it was – and Hansel pulled out his pipe and began to play.

Now the pipe was a fairy pipe, and whoever heard

it was obliged to dance, whether one liked or not. So the old witch was forced to dance a jig, on and on without rest, and could not stop to reach the rose. As Hansel did not cease playing for a moment the thorns tore the clothes from her body, and pricked her sorely, and at last she stuck quite fast.

Then Gretel set herself free once more, and she and Hansel set out for home. After walking a long way, Gretel grew tired, so they laid themselves down to sleep in a hollow tree that grew in a meadow near the woods. As they slept the witch – who had managed to get out of the prickly bush – came by; and, seeing her wand, was glad to lay hold of it. At once she turned poor Hansel into a fawn.

When Gretel woke and found what had happened she wept bitterly over the poor creature. The tears rolled down his eyes, as he laid himself beside her.

Gretel said, "Rest in peace, dear fawn; I will never leave you."

She took off her long golden necklace and put it round his neck, then she plucked some rushes and braided them into a string, and led the poor fawn by her side wherever she went.

At last one day they came to a little cottage; and Gretel, seeing that it was quite empty, said, "We can live here."

She gathered leaves and moss to make a soft bed for her fawn; and every morning she went out and plucked nuts and berries for herself, and shrubs and tender grass for her friend. The fawn ate out of her hand, and played and frisked about her. In the evening, when Gretel was tired, she laid her head on the fawn and slept; and if only poor Hansel could have had his right form again they would have led a very happy life.

After living for years in the woods by themselves until Gretel was a grown maiden, it chanced that the King came one day to hunt there. When the fawn heard the echoing of the horns, the barking of the dogs, and the shouts of the huntsmen, he wished very much to see what was going on.

"Oh, sister!" said he, "let me go out into the woods. I can stay no longer."

He begged so long that at last she let him go.

"But," said she, "be sure to come back in the evening. I shall shut the door to keep out the huntsmen, but if you tap and say, 'Sister, let me in,' I shall know you. If you do not speak, I shall keep the door fast."

Then away sprang the fawn, frisking and bounding along in the open air. The King and his huntsmen saw and followed the beautiful creature, but could not overtake him; for just as they thought they were sure of their prize he would spring over the bushes and be out of sight at once.

When it grew dark the fawn came running home to the hut and tapped, saying, "Sister, let me in!" Then Gretel opened the door, and in he jumped, and slept soundly all night on his soft bed.

Next morning the hunt went on; and when he heard the huntsmen's horns the fawn said, "Sister, open the door for me; I must go."

When the King and the huntsmen saw the fawn with the golden collar they again gave chase. The chase lasted the whole day, but at last the huntsmen surrounded him, and one wounded him in the foot, so that he became lame and could hardly crawl home. The man who had wounded him followed behind and heard the little fawn say, "Sister, let me in," upon which the door opened and shut again. The huntsmen went to the King and told him what he had seen and heard and the King said, "Tomorrow we will have another chase."

Gretel was very frightened when she saw that her dear fawn was wounded; but after washing the blood away she put some healing herbs on the place. In the morning there was nothing to be seen of the wound, and when the horn blew the little thing said, "I cannot stay here, I must go and look on; I will take care they don't catch me."

But Gretel said, "I am sure they will kill you this time: I will not let you go."

"I shall die of grief," said he, "if you keep me here." Then Gretel was forced to let him go: she opened the door with a heavy heart, and he bounded gaily into the woods.

When the King saw the fawn he cried to his men, "Chase him all day long till you catch him; but let no one do him harm."

At sunset, however, they had not been able to overtake him, and the King called the huntsmen, saying to the one who had watched, "Now show me the little hut."

So they went to the door and tapped, and the King said, "Sister, let me in."

The door was opened, and the King went in, and there stood a maiden more lovely than any he had ever seen.

Gretel was very frightened when she saw that it was not the fawn but a King with a golden crown who had entered her hut, but he spoke kindly and took her hand, and after they had talked awhile, he said, "Will you come with me to my castle and be my wife?"

"Yes," said Gretel, "I will go to your castle, but I cannot be your wife; and my fawn must go with me, for I cannot part with him."

"Well," said the King, "he shall come and live with you all your life, and shall want for nothing."

Just then in sprang the little fawn, and Gretel tied the string to his neck, and they left the hut together.

Then the King lifted Gretel on to his prancing horse and they rode to his palace, the fawn running behind them. On the way Gretel told the King her story. He knew the old witch and her wicked ways and sent for her, commanding her sternly to change the fawn into human form again.

When she saw her dear brother restored, Gretel was so grateful to the King that she at once consented to marry him. They lived happily all their days, and Hansel became the King's chief advisor.

PUSS IN BOOTS

here was once an old miller who had three sons. When he knew that he was about to die he called his sons to the bedside and divided his property among them. This was not very difficult in one way, because he had only three possession, his mill, his donkey, and his cat, and yet no one would say that the division he made was quite fair.

The eldest son had the mill. He was well off enough, for the farmers and nearby friends would give him plenty of work; and with industry and honesty he could look to becoming a rich man.

The second son, though not so lucky, had a useful, steady servant, though he hardly saw how he could depend on the donkey for his living. A donkey is very well as far as it goes; the difficulty is to make it go far enough. The miller's second son had, however, some hopes of getting employment from his brother, who would require a beast of burden to carry the sacks of corn to the mill and the sacks of flour back to the customers.

But the third son was in a sorry plight, and really it did not seem that the miller had been fair to him. True, it was a fine cat, with thick fur and a handsome tail, but, after all, a cat is only a cat! So the poor man sat down and wondered what he should do for a living; and the more he wondered the less able was he to come to a decision.

At last he began to moan aloud. "My brothers," he said, "by putting their property together and helping each other may do very well. There is always corn to be ground, and either sacks to be carried or odd jobs that a donkey can do. As for me, so far as I can see, when I have killed my cat, and made a fur cap or a pair of mittens of his skin, I shall have disposed of all my property, and must die of hunger."

The cat had been listening to every word his master said, and when he paused in his complainings, he came forward, and in a clear voice said, "Dear master, do not be so troubled. You had better not kill me; I shall be far more useful to you alive than dead."

"How can that be?" asked the young man, much surprised to find that he possessed a cat that could talk.

"If you will only give me a pair of boots and a sack," said Puss, "you shall have no cause for

Puss pulled on the boots as if he had been used to such things
all his life

The Ogre himself came to the door, carrying his great
spiked club

complaint."

The young man did not quite see how this would better his condition. However, he was so poor that he could hardly be worse off, and as the cat had always been very clever in catching rats and mice, he thought it best to see what Puss would do for him.

A bootmaker was sent for, and the miller's son managed to persuade him to delay any payment until Puss had brought in the promised fortune. The bootmaker took the measures very carefully, and when the boots came home the cat pulled them on as if he had been used to such things all his life. And very nice boots they were too, for the bootmaker had worked with a will and done his very best. The sack was easily secured from the mill, and this, too, met with Pussy's approval.

The next morning the cat rose with the sun, licked himself carefully all over, trimmed his whiskers, pulled on his fine new boots, hung the sack round his neck, and then crept to a rabbit-warren, taking care to keep out of sight of the bunnies. Here he opened his sack, into which he had put some bran and lettuce leaves, and, with the loose string in his hand, stretched himself out under a bush and pretended to be asleep.

He did not have to wait long. There are plenty of

foolish young rabbits in every warren, and presently a couple of giddy bunnies came hopping up, twitching their long ears. After sniffing at the opening of the sack for a moment or so, they hopped gaily in and began munching and nibbling the lettuce leaves as hard as they could, little thinking, poor simple things, of the fate that awaited them.

Master Puss had been watching with the mouth of the sack wide open, and his paws well on the string, ready to pull at the right moment.

Whisk! – the cat pulled the string, the sack closed, and the poor bunnies inside kicked frantically to be let out.

Master Puss lost no time in killing them, and, slinging the sack over his shoulder, set off to the palace, telling the guard at the gate that he wished to speak to the King.

Puss looked so fierce and determined as he twirled his whiskers that the sentries let him pass without any questions. He walked straight into the King's private room, and bowing gracefully and waving his tail, said:

"My master, the Lord Marquis of Carabas" – (this title was out of the cat's own head) – "presents his most dutiful respects to your Majesty, and has commanded me to offer his humble duty, and to assure your Majesty that among your subjects none is more devoted than my master." Here the cat made a very low bow, and the King wondered what was coming next.

The cat continued, "My master, the Lord Marquis of Carabas, humbly sends this small present of game for the gracious acceptance of your Majesty, as a slight token of the overflowing sense of affectionate veneration with which your Majesty has inspired him."

There was a speech for a cat to make!

The King, who was not so eloquent as his visitor, could not help feeling impressed by the beautiful long words the cat used. He had never heard of the Marquis of Carabas, but being polite – as all kings learn to be – he did not like to say so and answered graciously, "Tell my Lord Marquis that I accept his present with great pleasure, and am much obliged to him."

At the same time he could not help wondering how it was that he had never heard of the Marquis before. But Pussy's face wore such a look of sincerity that not the slightest shadow of suspicion that he was being imposed upon entered his kingly mind. Certainly the fine airs and manner of speech of the cat seemed to show that he belonged to a master of high degree.

All this was certainly very clever of the cat; but it was only the beginning of what he meant to do to make his master's fortune.

Bowing again to the King and flourishing his tail, he retired with all the grace and air of a thorough-bred courtier.

A day or two afterwards, Puss went again with his boots and his sack to try his fortune in the chase. This time a couple of young partridges, unused to the world and its ways, poked their beaks into the trap, and were quickly bagged and killed. These the cat also presented to the King as coming from the Lord Marquis of Carabas; and the speech he made was so eloquent, and had so many long words in it, that we had better not attempt to write it down but must leave you to imagine its beauty.

For some time the cat continued to bring a present of game to the King every day or two. His Majesty was so pleased that he gave orders that Puss should be taken down to the kitchen and given something to eat and drink whenever he called. While enjoying this good fare the faithful creature would contrive to speak to the royal servants of the large preserves and abundant game which belonged to his noble master.

Hearing one day that the King and his lovely daughter were going to take a drive by the riverside,

Puss concocted a very clever scheme.

Rushing into his master's presence, he said, "Go and bathe in the river, dear master, and I will make your fortune for you. Only bathe in the river, and leave the rest to me."

The so-called Marquis did not see how he was to make his fortune by bathing; but by this time he was so impressed by the cat's cleverness that he would have done anything Puss told him. As he was bathing, the King drove by with his daughter, the loveliest and most beautiful Princess in the world.

As soon as the royal carriage came in sight, Puss began to run to and fro, wringing his paws and tossing them wildly over his head, while he cried at the top of his voice:

"Help! help! help! my Lord Marquis of Carabas is drowning! Come and h-e-l-p my Lord – Marquis – of –Car-ra-ba-a-as!"

Hearing this pitiful wail, the King looked out of the carriage window; and, recognizing the cat who had brought him so many presents of game and made such beautiful speeches, he at once ordered his guards to go to the assistance of the Lord Marquis.

But this was only the beginning of the cat's scheme. Knowing that his master's shabby clothes would never do for a Marquis, he had hidden them under a big stone. He now ran to the carriage window and said to his Majesty:

"My Lord Marquis's clothes have been stolen while he was bathing, and the Marquis is shivering very much, with nothing to put on. He would like to wait upon your Majesty and the illustrious Princess, but of course he cannot do so without clothes."

"Oh," said the King with a laugh, "we'll soon remedy that."

He thereupon ordered a suit from his own wardrobe to be brought for the Marquis.

It is an old saying that fine feathers make fine birds; and the young miller certainly looked very well indeed in his new garments, as he came up to the carriage to thank the King for his kindness. His Majesty was so taken with him that he insisted that my Lord Marquis should come into the carriage and drive with them; and the beautiful Princess looked as if she were not at all displeased with the idea.

The young man felt rather bashful in his new position. But this was perhaps to his advantage; for the old King thought he was silent out of gratitude at the honour of being asked to ride in the King's carriage, while the lovely daughter for her part had no doubt the Marquis was speechless with admiration of her beauty. The King told a number of very long stories as they rode along; and as the Marquis said, "Yes, your Majesty," to everything, and seemed much interested, the King was perfectly satisfied, and thought him a well-informed and modest young man. The fact was, the Marquis was thinking all the time of the scrape he had got into, and wondering what the King and his lovely daughter would say to that rogue Puss if they only knew how he had tricked them.

But Puss was not the cat to leave his master in the lurch. He knew that people judge by appearances; and he had determined that his master should appear a wealthy man.

As soon as he had seen the young man safely seated in the King's carriage, he struck across the fields by a short cut and soon got a long way in advance of the royal party. In a wheatfield a party of reapers were gathering in the harvest. The cat ran up to them, and doubling his paws in a most expressive manner, said:

"Now, good people, if you don't say, when the King asks, that this field belongs to the Lord Marquis of Carabas you will all be chopped up into mincemeat."

The reapers, startled by the appearance of the fierce little booted creature, promised at once to do as they were told.

Soon afterwards the royal carriage passed, and the King stopped, as the cat had supposed he would. Beckoning one of the reapers, the King asked to whom all that fine wheat belonged.

The good people, remembering the threats Puss had made, replied:

"To the Marquis of Carabas, your Majesty."

"You have a fine crop of wheat, my Lord Marquis," said the King; "I am rather a judge of wheat."

"Yes, your Majesty," replied the Marquis; and the King thought again what a nice young man he was.

Meanwhile the cat came to a meadow where the mowers, with their scythes, were cutting the long grass.

"Good people," said Master Puss, running up, "when the King asks you presently to whom this meadow belongs, if you do not say 'To the Marquis of Carabas,' you will all be chopped up into mincemeat."

When the King passed he did not fail to ask to whom the fields belonged, and was much surprised at being answered again, "To the Marquis of Carabas, your Majesty."

"Really, my Lord Marquis, your possessions are

very great!" said the King; at which the young man blushed and answered, "Yes, your Majesty." And now the Princess thought he looked handsomer than ever. In fact, she was fast falling in love with him.

As they drove on the cat always ran before, saying the same thing to everybody he came across – that they were to declare the whole country belonged to his master.

But though the Marquis had no castle, there was a personage in those parts who had – and a fine castle it was. This personage was an Ogre, a giant, and a magician, all in one. The cat knew all about him and his wicked ways. Going boldly to the door, he rang a loud peal at the bell, and called out to the Ogre that he had come to pay a friendly visit and to inquire after his welfare. The cat did not really care about the giant's well-being, but the giant was the owner of much land, in fact, of those very fields and meadows which the cat had persuaded the workers to describe as belonging to the Marquis of Carabas. The Ogre himself came to the door, carrying his great spiked club. Bowing low, and doffing his plumed hat, Puss repeated his words and said he trusted the Ogre was now better. (The fact was, the Ogre had eaten a huntsman, top-boots and all, a few weeks before, and the spurs had disagreed with him.)

The Ogre replied that he was much obliged to the cat for his politeness, and invited him to walk inside. This was just what the cat wanted. He at once accepted the invitation, and, sitting on a table, began to talk to his host in his politest manner.

"Sir," he began, "everyone says you are a very clever magician."

"That is true," answered the Ogre, who was very vain.

"Sir," continued the cat, "I have heard that you are able to transform yourself into the shape of various animals."

"That also is true," answered the Ogre.

"But, sir," continued the cunning cat, "I mean large animals, such, for instance, as an elephant."

"Quite true," answered the Ogre. "See for yourself."

He muttered some magical words, and stood before the cat in the shape of an elephant, with large flapping ears, sharp tusks, little eyes, and long trunk – all complete.

The cat was startled at this sudden change; but, mustering courage, went on: "Well, sir, that is marvellous indeed! But can you change your shape at will, and represent whatever animal you choose?"

The Ogre wondered somewhat to find the cat so

anxious to obtain useful knowledge. But most people are flattered at being thought clever and like to exhibit their talents. So the Ogre resolved to gratify the curiosity of Puss.

The elephant waved his trunk three times in the air, and then stood before the astonished cat in the shape of a huge African lion, with a waving mane, a huge head, and the most awful set of big white teeth. The cat stood gazing at him like a creature transfixed with fright, just as he, in his time, had seen many a poor mouse terrified and trembling, and unable from very fear to fly from danger.

When the lion opened his mouth and gave a roar, the cat was so awestruck that he dashed straight up the wall, and, reaching a window, escaped on to the roof of the castle. His polished boots were very much in the way, but terror lent him wings, or rather feet, and his boots scarcely received a moment's thought. There he stood on the roof, quaking, and yet spitting and snarling, as it is cat nature to do, while every hair on his tail rose on end with horror. He could hear the Ogre below laughing at the thought of how he had frightened his visitor.

But presently Puss recovered courage, for he was a very brave cat, and felt ashamed of himself for having been so easily frightened. He knew by the laugh that the Ogre had now resumed his natural shape, so he came down again into the room with a cool and collected air, muttering something about the heat of the room, which had compelled him to run out for a breath of fresh air. At this the Ogre laughed louder than ever, but the cat sat down again on the table, and resumed the conversation as if nothing had happened.

"Sir," he went on, "I should not have believed these wonders if I had not seen them with my own eyes. You are the greatest magician it has ever been my good fortune to meet."

The Ogre made a deep bow and seemed much gratified.

"I have long heard of your fame and skill, but what I have seen far surpasses all my ideas of what a magician could achieve."

Here the Ogre again bent forward and made a deep bow. He was beginning to think the cat really had a good deal of sense after all.

"But once," went on Puss, "I heard of a conjuror who could not only assume the shape of a large animal like an elephant or a lion, but that of the smallest also – for instance, he would appear as a rat or a mouse. But then, you know, he was an old magician, who had been practising for a great

number of years, and I do not expect ever to find anyone who could come up to him."

"Don't you, indeed!" cried the Ogre angrily. "You
fancy he was a greater man than I? Ha! ha! – I'll
show you that I can do the same thing."

In a second or two, the Ogre was capering about
the room in the shape of a little mouse. This was
exactly what the cat wanted.

He instantly sprang on the mouse, and a single nip
with his sharp teeth put an end to the Ogre.

The cat, cunning fellow, had now gained his
object. Here was a castle for the Marquis of Carabas
– a sumptuous mansion in which no King need be
ashamed to rest after a long ride. And, the cat
thought, with glee, how surprised the Marquis would
be on his arrival.

Sure enough, just as Puss sat slyly licking his lips
after swallowing the Ogre, the King's carriage came
into sight.

The cat had only just time to run upstairs and
dress in a page's doublet when the King's coach
appeared in front of the castle.

There, to the great surprise of the Marquis of
Carabas, stood Puss, gallantly attired, and looking as
much at his ease as if he had done nothing but look
after the castle all his life. Not only did his clothes

give him a very dignified air, but he wore them with a grace which greatly increased their effect; and nothing could exceed the courtly air with which he welcomed the King and Princess to the castle.

"Welcome, your Majesty and your Royal Highness," he said, bowing low, "to the poor castle of my master, the Lord Marquis of Carabas! If your Majesty and the gracious Princess will be pleased to alight and take some refreshment, this will indeed be the proudest day of my life, and of my master's."

He made another deep bow, waved his cap, and laid his paw upon his heart.

"Upon our royal word, my Lord Marquis," cried the King, "you have a splendid castle, and we shall have great pleasure in viewing it more closely. We are always happy to visit our loving subjects; and moreover, shall be glad to stretch our royal legs; also our long ride has given us an appetite." (The King said this as a hint that some luncheon would be acceptable, and the sly cat took the hint, as you will see.) "What say you, daughter? Will you join us?"

The Princess, whose curiosity had been raised by the aspect of the castle, was quite willing; and the King commanded the Marquis to give the Princess his hand and conduct her into his dwelling.

Puss led the way, walking backward and bowing

with the grace and ease of a lord chamberlain.

The castle was splendidly furnished, for the Ogre had been a person of taste. Every room was hung with costly tapestry, and in the stables were a number of fine horses and a grand gilded coach in which the King himself would not have disdained to ride. Indeed, the Princess, after looking at it attentively and trying the cushions, went so far as to remark smilingly that it was very comfortable and that it seemed fit for a married couple. At this the cat nudged his master to make a bow.

While they were walking through the upper rooms, the cat slipped away for a few minutes to the kitchen. Here he looked quickly into the various cupboards and was delighted to find everything he wanted.

When the royal party returned to the great hall – lo and behold! – he had spread a grand luncheon.

The Marquis invited the King to be seated, and himself handed the Princess to a chair. If the King had been in a good mood before, he was radiant now; for he was rather fond of his meals, and the luncheon was faultless, the Ogre having made a point of having the best of everything.

With each glass of wine the King became more jovial, and appeared to conceive a greater affection for the Marquis. At last he began to treat him almost as a father might a son, and after luncheon he said:

"It will be your own fault, my Lord of Carabas, if you do not become our son-in-law, provided, of course, our daughter has no objection."

At this plain speech the young lady became scarlet with confusion, but she made no objection and did not look displeased. Indeed, she had long ago made up her mind that the Marquis was the handsomest and most attractive young man she had ever met.

So the Marquis of Carabas made a little speech (not nearly so fine as the cat could have made it for him), in which he thanked the King for his condescension, and expressed himself still more glad that the Princess had been graciously pleased to offer no objection; and as it was generally supposed that silence gave consent, he supposed it to be the case and he accepted it accordingly.

As for the cat, he was obliged to go into the courtyard to hide his joy, which was so great that he stood on his head on the flagstones and kicked his hind legs in the air.

Little more remains to be told. The Marquis returned with the King and the Princess to the royal palace; and the marriage took place a few days later amid great rejoicings.

The marriage took place amid great rejoicings

The Mandarin raised an alarm and ran after the lovers

THE WILLOW-PATTERN PLATE

any, many hundreds of years ago, there lived in China a very powerful Mandarin who, by inflicting unfair taxes and fines on the poor people he governed, had made a large fortune.

Having gained as much wealth as he wished, and fearing his evil ways would soon be found out, he sought leave from the Emperor to retire. He built himself a splendid riverside palace, where he spent his days in feasting and fancy living.

Now this Mandarin had an only daughter, a pretty, black-haired girl named Coo-Ee. He was very proud of her; and it was the dearest wish of his heart that she should marry some rich lord.

The Mandarin's secretary, a handsome young man named Chang, happened one day to be passing through the palace gardens and met Coo-Ee. Directly he set eyes on the maiden he fell in love.

And Coo-Ee, who had never seen so fine and handsome a young man before, fell in love with him too. The young people knew quite well that the old

Mandarin would never allow his pretty daughter to wed a poor secretary, but they loved each other so much that they felt they would rather die than be parted.

Every evening, as the sun went down, Coo-Ee, attended by her faithful handmaid, would meet Chang in some sheltered part of the gardens, and they would wander hand in hand through the orange-groves and by the placid waters of the lake, telling each other of their love.

One day a spying servant told the Mandarin of the lovers' meetings. He was in a great fury, and drove Chang from the house, declaring that if he ever attempted to see Coo-Ee again he should surely die.

The lovely Coo-Ee was then shut up in a set of rooms behind the banquet-hall; and as these rooms were surrounded on three sides by water, and had no outlet except through the banquet-hall, where the Mandarin sat nearly all day long, Coo-Ee could hardly stir without his knowledge. He dismissed her handmaid, and put an ugly, cross old woman in her place.

But not wishing to spoil his daughter's beauty by depriving her of fresh air, he caused a balcony to be built, jutting out over the water's edge, where she could lounge in the sunshine.

The Mandarin soon afterwards betrothed his daughter to a rich lord, who was old and ugly, and very disagreeable. Coo-Ee was told that, whether she liked it or not, when the peach-trees bloomed in spring, her marriage would take place.

Poor Coo-Ee was very miserable indeed, and spent her days in weeping and sighing.

No news came from Chang, but she did not despair, for as they were parted, the young man had managed to whisper, "Do not fear, dear one. You shall never be wedded to another whilst I live. I may not be able to come at once, but be sure that I shall come in time to save my own true love! Trust me, and all will yet be well!"

But as the weeks sped by and no message came from Chang, Coo-Ee grew very sad, and all her pretty smiles vanished.

"Surely he is dead," she said again and again.

One day, as she stood on her little balcony overlooking the lake, she noticed on the water below a tiny boat made of half a coconut shell, and fitted with a little sail that sent it merrily forward. Leaning over the edge, she managed to reach the boat with her sunshade. Within the shell was a folded note which proved to be a message from Chang. He told her he had heard of her coming marriage with the rich lord, and that if it ever came to pass he would certainly die.

At this Coo-Ee wept, but presently, drying her tears, she wrote a hopeful and loving little message in reply, bidding her lover not to despair, but to try and save her.

Putting her message in the little boat, she set a lighted joss-stick at one end, and launched it on the water. The light burned steadily, and the little vessel sailed out of sight without mishap. Coo-Ee took this for a good omen, and hope bloomed anew in her heart.

But for many days no further message came from Chang. When at last the willow-blossoms faded, and the buds on the peach-trees began to unfold, she despaired again.

One bright morning the Mandarin came into her room bearing a beautiful box of jewels, which he said was a present from the rich lord, who was coming that very day to feast with him, and to see his future bride.

"Take them away!" cried Coo-Ee, bursting into tears. "I will not marry him for all the jewels in the world! I will marry none but my beloved Chang!"

"Never dare to mention that rogue in my presence again!" roared the Mandarin. "He will never be your husband, for you shall marry the Ta-jin tomorrow! He will be here in a few hours, and will ask to see you after he has feasted on the good things I have had prepared for him. So let your maids dress you in your finest robes, and deck you with the jewels your future husband has sent you, and dry those tears at once or it will be the worse for you!"

When the wedding toilet was completed, the maids further adorned her with the Ta-jin's jewels, and declared that never had so beautiful and richly dressed a bride been seen before. But Coo-Ee refused to be comforted, and waited in her chamber, her hands folded in her lap, the picture of misery.

Shortly afterwards the Ta-jin arrived, gaily dressed servants going before him, beating gongs and shouting his praises, as was the custom in those days when great lords went visiting.

He was dressed most gorgeously, and wore a broad grin on his ugly face as he thought of the beautiful bride he was soon to marry.

The Mandarin received his visitor with pride, leading him at once to the banquet-hall, where a splendid feast had been set. The revellers drank so much wine, and grew so merry, that they forgot all else, and, indeed, toward evening could scarcely keep their eyes open. So when at dusk a stranger came to the door no one took the slightest notice of him, and he managed to step inside quite unseen by the servants.

This stranger was none other than Chang, the faithful lover. Looking around, he hastily threw on a servant's robe, and then drew a light screen across the entrance to the banquet-hall. He was thus able to step past and enter the room beyond.

In another moment the lovers were in each other's arms.

"We must fly at once," cried Chang.

Coo-Ee gave him the casket of jewels sent her by the Ta-jin, and then, wrapping a dark cloak over her wedding robe, she followed him as he crept softly behind the screen and down the steps into the garden beyond.

But now the Mandarin chanced to look from the window and caught sight of the fugitives. He raised an alarm, and, snatching his whip, ran after the lovers, shouting to them to stop. But they paid no heed and flew over the bridge, as you may see in any willow-pattern plate. Coo-Ee leads, carrying a spinner which she had snatched up ere she left, to show she did not mean to be an idle wife; the second figure is Chang, bearing the casket of jewels; and last comes the angry Mandarin, brandishing his whip.

Luckily for the lovers, the Mandarin, having feasted so long, could not move very quickly; so they had no great difficulty in out-running him and getting safely across the water.

When the Mandarin returned to the banquet-hall and told his guest what had happened, the Ta-jin flew into a great rage, and vowed to be revenged, declaring that Chang should be executed as a common thief for having run away with his jewels. Soldiers and servants were at once sent in every direction to hunt for the missing pair, but all their efforts proved in vain, for Coo-Ee's former handmaid had met them on the other side of the river, and taken them secretly to her home.

If you look on the left of the plate you will see her little house. Here Coo-Ee and Chang were married, and for a few days lived in peace. But soon their hiding-place was discovered, and late one evening the soldiers came knocking at the door.

The lovers were now in great danger, for the soldiers were at the front, and the house was surrounded by the river on all other sides. The handmaid ran to the door to ask the men their business, and thus gained a few precious moments, during which Chang leapt through the back window into the river. Coo-Ee watched him struggling with the water, swollen high with rain; but shortly, to her great joy, he returned with a boat, which had been kept in readiness.

When the soldiers rushed into the house they found no trace of the lovers, and, though they suspected that the pair had got away by the river, it was too dark to be certain.

The lovers floated swiftly down the stream. If you look at the willow-plate you will see the boat, with Chang at the prow, whilst Coo-Ee sleeps in the cabin.

Before daylight they had reached a great river, where many fine vessels of all kinds were to be seen. Here they sold one of their jewels, and with the money bought food and other necessities. For many days and nights afterward they went on far down the river toward the sea.

Presently they reached a small island where they thought it would be quite safe to remain. Chang crossed to the mainland, and by selling some more of the Ta-jin's jewels was able to buy the island. Then he set to work to build a house.

As the years passed Chang grew quite rich, for he cultivated his little island so well that it bore rich crops. Indeed, he became quite a famous farmer, and wrote a very learned book telling people how their land could be made to yield more crops.

Although Chang's book brought him fame, it also led to a great danger, for through its means his ancient enemy learned where he was. Gathering a great band of soldiers, the wicked Ta-jin sent them to attack the happy island-home.

The peaceful dwellers on the river could do little to defend themselves; and though Chang fought bravely, he was quickly slain by a soldier's spear. Seeing her beloved husband fall dead, Coo-Ee, filled with despair, and preferring to die rather than fall into the hands of the Ta-jin, set her room on fire and perished in the flames.

In pity for their sad fate, the good fairies, it is said, caused the spirits of the lovers to take the forms of two immortal doves, and these still float through the world, side by side, the emblems of a love which death itself could not destroy.

The wicked old Ta-jin, as a punishment, was afflicted with a horrible disease which soon brought him to a wretched end.

Now, when you look at any willow-pattern-plates you will be able to follow the story, which children in China and many other lands have loved for ages.

JACK THE GIANT KILLER

ong ago, in the reign of King Arthur, there lived in Cornwall, near the Land's End, a boy named Jack, who was the only son of a poor farmer.

Jack was a bold, fearless boy, and nothing delighted him more than to hear his father's stories about the Knights of the Round Table and their valiant deeds.

At this time there lived in England and Wales a number of giants. Big bullying fellows, they had great arms and legs, and a bad habit of taking what did not belong to them, especially cattle and sheep. As one of these giants could as easily chop up a whole sheep as we could slice a lamb chop, and would think as little of consuming a whole ox as we should of eating a steak, you can fancy that the people whose property they made free with were far from pleased to see them.

If there was any giant whose death Jack's friends particularly desired, it was the one named Cormoran, a cruel monster who lived on St. Michael's Mount, a small hill that rises out of the sea near the coast of Cornwall. This Cormoran was eighteen feet high and nine feet round; so you can fancy the quantity of stuff it would take to make him a pair of trousers; and perhaps that was the reason why he generally wore none. He had an ugly face, and a huge mouth with pointed teeth that caused fear and horror in all who beheld them. This horrible giant used to come out of his cave whenever he was hungry, and that was very frequently, for his appetite was enormous. So when he walked through the sea at low tide right into Cornwall, people used to take good care not to be at home. However, he would rarely have his walk for nothing, for if he could not carry off the people themselves he would take away their cattle a dozen at a time, slinging them on a pole across his shoulder as a man might sling a dozen rabbits. How short a time this dozen lasted him, and how soon he came for more, was really amazing.

When he got tired of beef, he would vary his diet by taking three or four dozen sheep and hogs; these small animals he would string round his waist – the sheep bleating and the pigs squealing – to the great annoyance of the owners, who watched him at a distance and dared not interfere.

This had been going on for many years, so that Cormoran was a terror through all the countryside, and people were afraid even to mention his name.

At last there came a day when the giant behaved worse than usual, and Jack, young as he was, resolved to see what he could do to slay him.

He set about it like this.

Early one winter's evening he swam to St. Michael's Mount, pushing before him a raft on which he took a pickaxe, a shovel, a horn, and a dark lantern. It was quite dark by the time he reached the Mount; but in the giant's cave a light showed, and Jack could see Cormoran, who had just finished his supper, picking his teeth with a hedge-stake. All night long Jack worked by the light of his dark lantern, digging a deep pit before the giant's dwelling. By dawn he had made a great hole, twenty feet deep and twenty feet broad. Not wishing the giant to see the hole, he covered it with sticks and straw, and placed some of the earth over them, to make it look like solid ground. He then put his horn to his mouth and blew a loud blast as a challenge to the giant to come out and fight. Cormoran woke up from his sleep with a start; and, when he saw what a little fellow stood defying him, his rage was awful.

"You saucy villain!" he roared; "you shall pay

dearly for breaking my rest. I will broil you for breakfast!"

At this Jack only laughed, rousing the giant to further fury.

Seizing his great spiked club, the huge fellow strode down the hill. Jack stood perfectly still, without the least sign of fear. Then the giant stretched out his hand and was about to seize Jack, when he trod on the loose earth and sticks and tumbled headlong into the pit.

"Oho, Mr. Giant," cried Jack, looking into the pit, "what say you now? Will nothing serve you for breakfast this cold morning but broiling poor Jack?"

The giant, more enraged than ever, made such a mighty effort to get out of the pit that the whole mountain shook, and stones and rubbish came rolling down its sides into the hole. Jack saw there was no time to be lost. Raising his pickaxe, he struck Cormoran a blow on the crown which killed him at once.

Jack returned in triumph, and when the people heard of the giant's death they rejoiced greatly and could not say enough in praise of the farmer's brave son. The justices and great squires sent for him and declared that henceforth he should be called JACK, THE GIANT KILLER. As a further reward they gave him a handsome sword and a belt on which was embroidered in letters of gold:

THIS IS THE VALIANT CORNISHMAN
WHO SLEW THE GIANT CORMORAN.

Jack soon found that his title brought not only praise and fame but a good deal of danger. It frequently happens that success in one task only leads to new tasks and the necessity for still greater efforts. But Jack was so pleased with himself that he vowed he would kill every giant and ogre he could find.

It happened that there lived among the mountains of Wales a great hulking fellow who had been a special friend of Cormoran's, and had often been invited by him to dine off a couple of oxen or half a dozen sheep. When he heard of Cormoran's death this giant, Blunderbore by name, was very angry, and vowed vengeance against Jack should he ever have him in his power.

Nothing daunted, Jack took a journey into Wales; and one day, as he was walking through a woods, sat down beside a fountain to rest. The day was hot, and Jack, overcome by fatigue, quickly fell asleep. As he lay there peacefully sleeping, dreaming perhaps of his victory over Cormoran, he had little idea of the peril into which he had fallen. For this was an enchanted forest, and nearby, in an enchanted castle, lived old Blunderbore. While Jack slept, the giant came to the fountain for water, and as the words on Jack's belt showed clearly who he was, Blunderbore was greatly delighted.

"Aha!" he chuckled; "have I caught you, my valiant Cornishman? Now you shall pay for your tricks." He lifted the sleeping Jack on his shoulder and strode off towards his castle. The jolting woke Jack from his sleep: and you may be sure that even so brave a lad felt not a little alarmed when he found himself in Blunderbore's clutches.

The giant soon arrived at his castle, and Jack was still more alarmed when he looked round, for on the floor were strewn the skulls and bones of many men and children who had been devoured by this cruel ogre. Blunderbore seemed to enjoy Jack's fright, and told him with a horrid grin that his favourite food was men's hearts eaten with salt and pepper, and he showed pretty plainly that Jack's heart would form a part of one of his next meals.

But Blunderbore did not care to eat such a nice dish as the Giant Killer all by himself, and went off to fetch one or two friends to supper, leaving Jack securely locked in a room. While he was away Jack heard dreadful shrieks, groans and cries from many parts of the castle, and presently a deep mournful voice solemnly chanted these lines:

"Haste, valiant stranger, haste away,
Or you'll become the giant's prey.
On his return he'll bring another,
Still more savage than his brother –
A cruel, horrid monster who,
Before he kills, will torture you –
Haste, valiant stranger, haste away,
Lest you become the giant's prey."

These dreadful warnings and the horrible sights he had seen for a time took all the pluck from Jack, but he was not one to give way to despair. He ran to the window to see if he could discover any means of getting away. A single glance showed that he would never be able to leap out. The window was too high for him and, moreover, was right over the gate of the castle. Then – horror! – he saw the two giants coming along arm-in-arm, grinning and chuckling as they thought of the feast in store for them.

In utter despair, Jack glanced round the room. To his great joy, in a far-off corner he saw two stout

Jack saw a giant dragging along a knight and his lady by the
hair of their heads

Putting on his shoes of swiftness, Jack began to run from the
double-headed giant

ropes. To seize them, make a running noose at the end of each, and twist them firmly together, was the work of a moment; and just as the giants were entering the gate of the castle, he cleverly dropped a loop over the head of each. The middle of the rope he had already passed over a beam of the ceiling, and he now pulled and hauled with all his might, pulled with such a will, indeed, that the giants were soon black in the face. When his enemies were half strangled and had not much strength left, Jack clambered out of the window, and, sliding down the rope, drew his sword and killed them both.

Having saved himself from a cruel death, Jack's first thought was for the other prisoners. Indeed, they seemed to know by some means that the tyrants were dead, and fearing Jack would hurry from the dreadful place and leave them to their fate, they all called out to him. With difficulty Jack managed to drag from its hiding-place the giant's great bunch of keys and soon had all the captives free. On going through the rooms and dungeons, he came upon three unfortunate ladies tied up by the hair of their heads and almost starved to death. Their husbands, they said, had been killed and eaten by the giants and they had been awaiting a like fate.

"Ladies," said Jack, "this cruel monster and his

brother will never trouble you more, for I have put an end to them. I give you this castle and all the riches it contains so that you may have some amends for the sufferings you have endured."

He thereupon gave them the keys, and, bidding them a polite goodbye, resumed his journey into Wales.

He walked on sturdily till night came, by which time he had lost his way in a lonely valley between two high mountains. At last he reached a large and handsome house, which looked very inviting to a weary man who had walked many miles after killing two giants. He knocked boldly at the door to ask admittance for the night, and was rather startled when the door was opened by a large two-headed giant. This monster was indeed more to be dreaded than the others; for he was not fierce in the way he behaved, like Cormoran or Blunderblore, who by threats and boastings put an enemy on his guard, but cunning, and generally effected by tricks and stratagem what others did by open violence. At the same time, even in appearance, he might be thought an alarming fellow. He was as tall as Cormoran and a foot or two broader round the waist. In his two heads he had, of course, two mouths, and perhaps that is why he was so fat.

He spoke very politely to Jack, and when he heard he had lost his way invited him into the house, gave him a good supper, and sent him to bed. Jack, however, did not like the appearance of the giant, one of whose heads used to look at the other out of the corners of the eyes, which then winked in a very artful manner. Jack thought, too, he had seen the giant shaking his fist at him slyly once or twice during supper; so, instead of going to sleep, he listened. Presently he heard the giant marching about in the next room, singing a duet all by himself – the treble with one mouth, the bass with the other. This was the song he sang:

> *"Though here you lodge with me this night,*
> *You shall not see the morning light;*
> *My club shall dash your brains out quite!"*

"Oho!" said Jack softly, when he heard this pleasant ditty. "Are these the tricks you play upon visitors? I shall prove a match for you yet." Groping about the room, he found a thick log of wood in the fireplace; he put this into the bed and covered it up well, after which he concealed himself in a dark corner.

In the middle of the night the giant came creeping

into the room, nodding his two heads at each other with a knowing wink. He sidled up to the bed, and – "Whack! – whack! – whack!" – down came his cruel club upon the log of wood, just where Jack's head would have been but for his clever trick.

The giant, thinking he had broken all the bones in his guest's body, retired well pleased with himself, and lay down on his own bed to sleep.

Fancy how surprised he was when, early in the morning, he heard Jack stirring in his room, singing gaily, and apparently in the best possible spirits.

When Jack came calmly into the room and thanked him for his nice night's lodging, the giant rubbed his four staring eyes and pulled his hair to make sure he was awake.

"How-ow-w-w did you sle-e-e-p?" stammered the giant at last. "Did anything dist-u-r-r-b you in the night?"

"Oh, I slept very well," replied Jack. "I believe a rat came and gave me three or four slaps with his tail, but he soon went away again."

The giant was so surprised that he sat on a bench, and scratched his heads for three minutes, trying to make things out. Then he rose slowly, and went to prepare breakfast.

Jack now thought he would play the giant another

trick. Taking a great leather bag, he fastened it under his tunic, his idea being to make the giant believe he could eat as much as himself. From the readiness with which he had believed the story about the rat, Jack was not inclined to think much of the giant's brains, even though there were two heads to keep them in.

Presently the giant came in with two great bowls of hasty pudding, and began feeding each of his mouths by turns. Jack took the other bowl and pretended to eat the pudding it contained; but, instead of swallowing it, he kept stowing it in the great leather bag. The giant stared harder than ever, wondering that such a little chap as Jack could eat so much.

"Now," said Jack, when breakfast was over, "I will show you a trick. I can cut off my head, my arms, or my legs and put them on again, just as I choose, and do a number of strange and wonderful things besides. Look here, I will show you an instance." So saying, he took hold of a knife, ripped up the leather bag, and all the hasty pudding came tumbling on the floor, to the great surprise of the giant.

"Ods! splutter hur nails!" cried the giant in his Welsh way, "hur can do that hurself." Determined not to be outdone by such a little chap as Jack, he seized his knife! plunged it into the place where his hasty pudding was, and dropped down dead.

After this clever achievement Jack had a better right than ever to the name of "Giant Killer." He continued his journey, and a few days afterwards we find him staying in very grand company indeed.

The only son of good King Arthur had a great liking for adventures, which he no doubt inherited from his father, for King Arthur in his time fought many combats and overcame many foes, never sheathing his sword without winning. Now, the Prince had at this time visited Wales on an errand somewhat similar to Jack's. He wanted to deliver a beautiful lady from the hands of a wicked magician who was keeping her in captivity. When Jack found that the Prince had no servants, he begged leave to attend him, and the Prince, seeing by the inscription on the belt who the sturdy man was, very gladly consented.

The Prince was very brave and handsome; but, like many other Princes, had a habit of giving away and squandering his money without waiting till he had got any more. One day the Prince had played this game with such goodwill that when night came he had not a silver penny left to pay his lodging.

"What shall we do?" he asked Jack with a rueful face. "And how shall we provide ourselves with food for the rest of the journey?"

"Leave that to me, your Highness," said Jack, at which the Prince felt greatly comforted.

A mile or two farther on they came to a large castle, which they were told was inhabited by a very wonderful giant indeed, for he had three heads, and could fight five hundred men.

The Prince felt rather doubtful about asking such a monster to give them lodging and supper even for one night. "What shall we do there?" asked the Prince, "he can eat us up at a single mouthful; indeed, we shall hardly be a mouthful for him, and may but just fill his hollow tooth."

"My lord," said Jack, "do you wait here till I return and leave me to manage him." Jack accordingly went on alone, and knocked loudly at the gate.

"Who's there?" roared the giant.

"Only your poor Cousin Jack," came the answer.

The giant, like most great men, had a good many poor relations, and Jack guessed this very well.

"Dear uncle," he went on, "I have brought you news."

"What news, Cousin Jack?" asked the giant.

"Bad news, uncle," answered Jack.

"Pooh!" cried the giant; "what can be bad news for a person like me, who has three heads and can fight five hundred men and make them fly before me."

"Oh, my poor uncle!" cried cunning Jack, "the King's son is coming, with two thousand men, to kill you and destroy your castle!"

All the giant's three faces turned pale at once; and he said in a trembling voice, "This is bad news, indeed, Cousin Jack; I'll hide in the cellar, and you shall lock me in till the King's son has gone."

Jack laughed in his sleeve as he turned the key of the cellar upon the simple giant. Then he brought the Prince to the castle, and they feasted and enjoyed themselves.

Next morning Jack helped the Prince to a good share of the giant's gold and silver, and sent him three miles forward on his journey. He then went back to let his "uncle" out of the hole. The giant looked about him in a puzzled way, and seemed to think the two thousand men had not done so much damage to his castle after all, and that they had very small appetites. He then asked Jack what reward he would like for saving the castle, and Jack answered, "Good uncle, all I want is the old coat and cap and the rusty sword and the worn slippers which are at your bed's head."

"You shall have them," said the grateful giant: "they will be very useful to you. The coat will make you invisible; the cap of knowledge will reveal to you hidden things; the sword of sharpness will cut through the best coat of mail ever made; and the slippers will give you swiftness; take them, and welcome, my brave Cousin Jack."

Jack thanked the giant, as well he might, for such very useful gifts. Then he hurried after the Prince, and they soon reached the dwelling of the beautiful lady who was in the power of the wicked magician. She was very pleased to see the Prince, and gave a great feast to celebrate his arrival. At the end the lady rose and, waving her fine cambric handkerchief, said:

"My lord, you must submit to the custom of this place. Tomorrow morning I command you to tell me on whom I have bestowed this handkerchief, or you must lose your head."

She then left the room, and the young Prince went to bed very mournful and very puzzled at so strange a demand.

Jack, however, made light of the matter, for, having put on his cap of knowledge, he was aware that the lady was compelled, by the power of enchantment, to meet the wicked magician every night in the middle of the great forest. When the Prince had retired, Jack put on his invisible coat and the slippers of swiftness and was at the meeting-place before the lady arrived. When she came he saw her give the handkerchief to the magician, and with one blow from the sword of sharpness he cut off the rascal's head. At once the enchantment ended and the lady was restored to her former virtue.

The Prince married her the very next day, which perhaps you will think rather a quick proceeding; but they did all such things quickly in olden times. The happy pair then proceeded to King Arthur's Court, and so pleased was that monarch that he made Jack one of the Knights of the Round Table.

But Jack could not long remain idle; and, hearing that there were still many giants at large in Wales, he begged the King to provide him with a horse and money that he might go forth against them.

On the third day of his journey, passing through a thick forest, he heard the most doleful groans and shrieks. Making his way through the trees, he saw a great giant dragging along a handsome knight and a beautiful lady by the hair of their heads. Jack at once put on his invisible coat, and, taking his sword of sharpness, struck at the giant. The great monster was so huge, however, that Jack could not reach his body, but had to hack at his thighs. At last, putting forth all his strength, he managed to cut off both the giant's legs below the garters, and the great trunk came crashing down, making the trees tremble and the earth itself shake with the force of the fall. Setting his foot on the monster's neck, Jack plunged his sword into the body and giant rolled over dead.

The knight and his lady thanked their deliverer, you may be sure; but Jack would have done the same for anybody in distress, as a good knight is bound to do. Jack declined an invitation to go to their castle and live with them, for he wanted to see the giant's den, where, he was told, lived an even fiercer giant, brother to the one he had just slain.

"When I have killed him," said Jack, "I will return and pay my respects to you."

Mounting his horse, Jack rode on for about a mile and a half, when he saw above him the mouth of a great cavern. Here sat the giant, on a huge block of timber, with a knotted club by his side.

"Here is the other," cried Jack; and, having put on the invisible coat, he hit the giant a blow with his sword. Being in rather too great a hurry, however, Jack did no more than cut off the great fellow's nose. The giant gave a roar like claps of thunder and rolled his great eyes from side to side, but of course could not see who had struck him. So he took up his club and began to lay about him right and left, like one mad with pain and fury. This gave Jack the chance he wanted, and, slipping behind his enemy, he jumped on the great block of timber and so was able to reach the giant's head, which he soon cut off. This he sent to King Arthur with that of the giant's brother; the two heads just made a good wagon-load.

Now, at length, Jack felt entitled to go and see the knight and his lady; and there were rare doings at the castle. The knight and his guests drank to the health of the Giant Killer.

The mirth was at its height when a messenger arrived to say that Thundel, a fierce two-headed giant and a near relative of the two dead giants, was coming, burning with rage, to avenge his kinsmen's death. All was hurry and fright; but Jack bade every one be quiet – he would soon settle Master Thundel. First, he sent some men to cut the drawbridge over the moat, just leaving a slight piece of each side. The giant soon came running up, swinging his club, and though the knight and those with him had every confidence in Jack's courage and skill, they could not help feeling very anxious about the issue of the combat when they saw what a very great giant Thundel was, and how all the country people fled in terror before him, as he came tramping heavily along. It is true he could not see Jack – for our hero had taken the precaution to put on his coat of darkness – yet his sense of smell was so acute that as Jack approached across the bridge he knew someone was at hand and cried out:

> *"Fe! – fi! – foh! – fum!*
> *I smell the blood of an Englishman!*
> *Be he alive, or be he dead,*
> *I'll grind his bones to make my bread!"*

"Say you so, my friend?" asked Jack. "You are a monstrous miller indeed."

"Ah!" cried the giant, "I hear the voice of the villain who killed my kinsmen. I will tear thee with my teeth and grind thy bones to powder."

"First catch me," cried Jack; and, flinging off his coat of darkness, he put on his shoes of swiftness, and began to run, the giant taking great strides after him. Jack led him round and round the moat, and then suddenly darted across the drawbridge. The giant followed closely, but no sooner came to the middle, where the bridge had been cut, than it snapped with his weight, and down he went – splash! – into the moat, which was full of water and of great depth. The giant rolled about like a great whale, struggling fiercely to release himself.

A strong cart rope, with a running noose at the end, was now cleverly thrown over the giant's head by Jack, and the giant was drawn to the castle side of the moat, where, half drowned and half strangled, he lay at the mercy of the Giant Killer, who completed his task by cutting off the giant's double head, to the great delight of all the people in the castle.

After spending a short time very pleasantly with the knight and his lady, Jack again set out in search of adventures. He came one night to the foot of a high mountain, where stood a small and lonely house. Jack knocked at the door, and an old man, whose hair and beard were as white as snow, let him in and bade him welcome to such food and lodging as he could provide. It appeared that he was a hermit and lived all by himself in the hut. He did many good deeds among the people around, giving them medicine when they were sick, and advising them as to their concerns, so that all respected and loved him.

When the hermit discovered that Jack was the far-famed Giant Killer, he said, "I am rejoiced to see you, for you can do good service here. At the top of this mountain stands an enchanted castle, the dwelling of the Giant Galligantus. This wicked monster, by the aid of a magician as bad as himself, has now a number of knights and ladies in captivity, and the magician has changed them into the shape of beasts. Among the rest is a duke's daughter, who was seized as she was walking in her father's garden, and borne away to the castle in a chariot drawn by two fiery dragons. They have cruelly made her the shape of a deer. A great many knights have tried to break the enchantment and set her free, but fiery griffins are posted at the castle gate, who destroy all who come near. With your coat of darkness you might manage to pass by the fiery griffins which keep guard at the gate without being seen, and your sword of sharpness would do the rest."

Jack was at once eager to try the adventure, and the hermit added:

"I have heard that when you have once passed the griffins, you will find assistance in your adventure; for there is an inscription on the castle gates which will tell you how to break the enchantment, if you can only get so far."

Jack promised to do his very best; and early the next morning set off to climb the mountain, dressed in his invisible coat. It was well that he had put this garment on; for long before he got to the castle he could see the old magician, who was of a suspicious nature, looking out.

At the castle gate sat the two griffins, but, thanks

to his coat, Jack passed between them unharmed. On the gate hung a large golden trumpet, and below it were written these lines:

"Whoever can this trumpet blow,
Shall cause the giant's overthrow."

Jack at once seized the trumpet and blew a mighty blast that echoed far and near. Immediately the castle seemed to tremble and all the gates flew open. The giant and the magician knew their wicked lives would soon be over, and stood biting their thumbs and shaking with fear. Jack with his sword of sharpness despatched them both, and all the knights and ladies who had been changed into beasts at once resumed their proper shapes. More wonderful still, the castle vanished like smoke.

After resting that night at the old man's hermitage, the lords and ladies set off for the Court. Among them was the duke's daughter, and when King Arthur asked the Giant Killer to name the reward he would wish for his services, Jack humbly asked that the lady might be his wife. They were married amid great rejoicings. The King gave them a large estate, and they lived the rest of their days very happily, untroubled by giants.

"If you open that door," said Bluebeard, "I shall be very
angry indeed"

She touched it with her wand and it was changed at once into
a beautiful coach

As Cinderella left the ballroom one of her glass slippers fell off

On Cinderella's dainty little foot the slipper appeared to be a
skin of glass

CINDERELLA

nce upon a time there lived a worthy gentleman and his wife who had a pretty little baby girl. One sad day the mother died. A few years later the gentleman married again, and so the little girl, who was now fast growing up, had a stepmother. Unfortunately, this stepmother was proud, haughty, and deceitful, and had a bad habit of always wanting her own way. To make matters worse, she had two daughters who were as disagreeable as herself.

These girls were nearly ten years older than the gentleman's own little daughter, and the poor child began to lead a very dreary life among her new relations. At first they only slighted and teased her; but when they found she bore this treatment patiently they went from bad to worse.

In a very few months the good man became ill and died, and the little girl was left without a friend in the world.

As she grew up, the child became prettier and

prettier; and the prettier she became the more the sisters hated her. Her life was hard enough before, but now it became almost unbearable. She was treated worse than any servant, and made to do all the drudgery of the house. While the mother and the two elder sisters flaunted in silks and satins, the little girl was clothed in rags. She was compelled to eat any odd scraps that were left from the table and to sleep in a dark attic where there was only an old straw mattress and a broken chair.

When her household work was over for the day, the poor girl would go into the kitchen and sit down quietly by the chimney among the cinders. This habit procured for her the nickname of "Cinder-ella". So sweet and sunny was her nature, however, that she never complained of her hard lot, and went blithely about her work the whole day long, without once envying her cruel sisters.

But, however shabbily Cinderella was clothed, she always looked handsomer than the sisters, for all their fine things, and as the years went by she became more and more beautiful. This made her jealous step-sisters more unkind than ever, and they never tired of tormenting the poor girl. When they dressed themselves to go to balls and parties, Cinderella had to help them, and after she had taken the greatest pains they would reward her only with some harsh words as they went downstairs, or very likely with a blow.

One day the two sisters received a note on scented rose-tinted paper, which made them hold their heads up higher than ever. It was an invitation to a grand state dress ball to be given by the King's son. For six weeks before the date of the ball the sisters talked of nothing else but what they should wear. It was wonderful how these girls, usually so lazy, became all at once industrious. They took all their dresses from the wardrobes, and had long talks over every one in turn. Also they held a sort of review of all their jewels, which were many and costly, and scared their mother by buying many unnecessary new ones. At the same time they found plenty of work for Cinderella, who, after her household drudgery was done, had to find their fine linen and laces and to trim and sew for them; and when she had done her very best they only scolded her for her trouble.

When the day of the ball really came, there was a great hurry-skurry. The sisters, whose usual hour for rising was half-past ten, found they could very well get up at six; and a quarter past they rang for Cinderella. They continued to dress by easy stages all day long, except during a couple of hours in the middle of the day, which they spent in having their dinner and lying down for a nap. However, they found some work for Cinderella till they came back, so that the poor girl got no dinner at all that day.

As Cinderella was fastening the dress of one of the sisters, the other who sat by said, "Pray, Cinderella, would you not like to go to the ball?"

"Nay," replied poor Cinderella, "you are only mocking me. It is not for such as I to go to balls and parties."

"Very true," said the ill-natured girl; "people would stare, I dare say, to see a little cinder-wench at a ball."

That was all the return Cinderella got for her toil since six o'clock in the morning.

After all her pains the two sisters were not satisfied with their appearance, and declared that they looked terrible, which was true enough; but it was because they were full of pride and ill-nature, and not from any fault of Cinderella's. They drove off in a fine carriage, with a coachman and two footmen in handsome liveries; and Cinderella was left to retire to her dark, dismal, lonely kitchen.

For some time she stood thinking a little of her sisters' unkindness, and a great deal about the merry ball, to which she would have gladly gone. The more she thought the more sorrowful and sad she became, and at length she sat down in her chimney corner and began to cry. How long she sat she did not know; but she felt very tired and sleepy and sobbed herself into a doze.

When she opened her eyes she was surprised to see before her a beautiful lady, standing on a small cloud, a wand in her hand.

"My dear Cinderella," said the lady, "I am your Fairy Godmother."

Cinderella wondered at this, because she had never seen the lady before.

"I do not like to see you so unhappy: tell me why you are crying."

Cinderella could only sob out, "Because they treat me so badly, and are never satisfied – and – and –"

"And what, Cinderella?"

"And I do not like being here all by myself," answered the poor child, "and – and I want"

"You want to go to the ball, Cinderella; is it not so?"

Cinderella nodded.

"Well, go you shall. But first we must get a coach and horses to take you. Go into the garden and fetch me the largest pumpkin you can find, and if there are any mice in the trap you had better bring them also."

Cinderella was much surprised at this request, but at once did as she was told. The Fairy cut a hole in the pumpkin, just at the side, where the door of a real coach would be, and then scooped it out, leaving only the rind. Then she touched it with her wand, and it was changed at once into a beautiful coach of state, decked with scarlet and gold and lined with satin.

In the mouse-trap had been six of the sleekest and fattest mice you could wish to find, but they had somehow managed to make their way out and now sat in a row, looking up at the Fairy Godmother like so many children on a bench at school. The Fairy touched them one by one with her wand, and they turned into handsome horses, with arched necks, long tails, and splendid harness all plated with gold.

"Well, child," said the Fairy, "here are a carriage and horses at least as handsome as those of your sisters; but now we want a coachman. Go and see if there are any rats in the rat-trap."

Off tripped Cinderella, and soon returned in triumph, bearing the trap, in which was a large black rat with a fine beard. The Fairy touched it, and at once the rat became a handsome coachman with a splendid state costume embossed with gold. He climbed on to the coach-box, and sat there, the reins gathered in his hands, ready to start when his mistress was ready. Footmen were now required, and Cinderella was directed by the Fairy to bring in six lizards which she would find behind the garden watering-pot. A touch of the wonderful wand changed the four largest into tall footmen, with gorgeous costumes to match the coachman's; and the two small ones were turned into pages. The whole train of servants was now complete, and looked fit for any Princess: the pumpkin-coach shone like gold, the mice-horses tossed their heads and pranced, the rat-coachman was in his place, the four tall lizard-footmen jumped up and hung on to the footboard, while the lizard-pages were ready to open and close the carriage door; all of them sprang at once into their positions with the ease of practised servants.

"Well, Cinderella," said her Godmother, "are you not pleased with your carriage?"

"Yes, indeed," said Cinderella doubtfully; "But – " And she glanced at her ragged frock.

Her Godmother understood her meaning and laughed.

"You do not think you can go in those clothes, my dear? Neither shall you."

Once more the wand waved: in an instant Cinderella's shabby attire had changed to a beautiful robe of the loveliest rainbow tints, with precious stones here and there, and a beautiful rope of pearls. Her little feet were no longer bare but covered with silk stockings and a pair of beautiful slippers of spun glass, that glittered like diamonds.

"Now", said the Fairy to Cinderella, as she stood admiring her lovely clothes and carriage, "all you have to do is to get into this carriage and drive away. I hope you will enjoy yourself very much. But I have one thing to say. You must leave the palace before midnight; if you are there one second after the clock strikes twelve your coach will return to the form of a pumpkin, your coachman become a rat, your horses mice, your footmen and pages lizards, and you yourself will be the little cinder-wench you were a few minutes ago."

Cinderella, her heart full of joy, promised faithfully to leave the ball in good time. The footmen handed her into her coach, the coachman cracked his whip, and off they drove in grand style.

There was no small stir at the palace when the splendid carriage drove up, and great indeed was the interest displayed in Cinderella. News was quickly carried to the Prince that a beautiful Princess whom nobody knew had arrived. The Prince himself went out to receive her, and conducted her to the ballroom. As they passed everyone stood aside and people whispered, "How beautiful she is!" The Court ladies all took particular notice of her clothes, and some of them, thinking they had never seen so lovely a vision, resolved to have dresses made in exactly the same style. The Prince fell in love with her at once, and, to the annoyance of many of the ladies, would dance with no one else.

A grand supper was served, but the Prince was so very much in love that he could scarcely eat more than a single apple-tart and left untasted the very choicest ice-cream. As for Cinderella, she sought out her ugly sisters, whom nobody seemed to wish to speak to, and paid them all sorts of civil attentions, which, coming from so grand a lady, pleased and flattered them very much.

While she was talking to them the warning voice of the clock told eleven and three-quarters, and Cinderella, mindful of her Godmother's instructions, at once rose, and, with a graceful curtsey to the royal family, hastened to her carriage.

The Prince hurried after her, begging her to renew her visit on the following evening, and, when the carriage had gone, returned to the company very dull and quite bored by the festivities.

Cinderella arrived home in time to receive the approval of her Godmother and a promise that, as the invitation had been given, she should go to the ball again. While they were talking, a loud rap at the door announced the return of the two sisters. The Fairy Godmother vanished, leaving Cinderella sitting in the chimney-corner, rubbing her eyes and pretending to be vey drowsy.

"Ah," said the elder sister, hoping to excite Cinderella's envy, "it has been a most charming ball. A rich and beautiful Princess – the most lovely girl I have ever seen – was there, and she specially singled us out and was very polite and attentive to us both."

"Indeed!" said Cinderella, pretending to stifle a yawn, but really laughing to herself. "And who was this wonderful Princess?"

"Nobody knows," said the sister, "not even the Prince, who takes no pains to conceal that he is greatly in love with her."

"Really!" said Cinderella, smiling to herself again. "How beautiful she must be. I should love to see her. Will you not let me go tomorrow? You could lend me the yellow gown you wear on Sundays!"

"Really!" cried the sister, glaring in surprise. "How impertinent you are tonight! The idea of you going to the ball! Just mind your pots and pans, please, and leave balls and parties to your betters."

Cinderella accepted the rebuke with meekness, for

if her sister had really been good-natured enough to lend her the gown she would not have known what to do.

The next evening the two sisters again went to the ball, and Cinderella appeared shortly afterwards, even more splendidly dressed than on the first night.

"Now remember twelve o'clock," had been her Fairy Godmother's parting words, and Cinderella had readily promised. The Prince had been watching for her ever since the first carriage drew up. He never left her side the whole of the evening; would dance with no one else; and paid her such compliments that Cinderella's cheeks flushed and she hardly dared lift her eyes to his face.

But what with the dancing, the lights, the supper, and the Prince's attentions, time went very quickly, and she forgot her Godmother's words about the clock. Suddenly, just in the middle of one of the Prince's nicest speeches, the first stroke of twelve rang upon her ear. Up she started, and without even waiting to curtsey to the guests, ran from the ballroom as fast as she could. At the head of the stairs one of her glass slippers came off, but, fearful of what would happen, she dared not stop to put it on. As she reached the bottom stair she heard the last stroke of twelve; her beautiful gown fell from her, and she found herself clad once more in her dingy working-dress. The Prince hurried after her, but she was too quick for him. He caught sight of the glass slipper, however, and snatched it up. At the palace door all he saw was a poor dirty lass of whom no Prince could be expected to take the slightest notice.

Cinderella ran all the way home, and reached her house, panting and breathless and ragged, in very different style from the state in which she had left for the ball.

One thing she had, however, to remind her of her grandeur, and that was the other glass slipper, which had not disappeared with the rest of her fine attire.

She had barely slipped it into her pocket when she heard her sisters at the door.

She again met them rubbing her eyes, and with a weary yawn, asked how they had been entertained, and whether the beautiful Princess had been there. "Yes," they replied, adding that at twelve o'clock she had suddenly started up and left the ballroom. Nobody could tell what had made her run off in such a hurry, when just before she had been dancing gaily. Nobody could tell what had become of her, for the Prince and the guards had only seen a dirty little girl run out about that time, and she could not possibly be the Princess, for she looked like a cinder-sifter.

After that the Prince had seemed to lose all pleasure in the party, and everything flagged, so that the guests soon took their leave.

Cinderella listened without saying a word, turning her face to the kitchen fire, and perhaps it was this which made her look so rosy; but as nobody ever thought of noticing her at home it did not matter in the least.

Early the next morning she resumed her weary round of work and drudgery just as if nothing had happened.

The Prince dreamed all night of his beautiful partner, and rose the next morning still thinking of her. He lost all taste for the sports and amusements in which he had delighted, and grieved the old King, his father, by refusing even to take his meals as usual. All day long he lay stretched on a couch, thinking of the fair Princess. When he returned to his pillow at night, it was only to dream of her again. At last a bright idea struck him, and he hurriedly ordered a herald to ride through the city and proclaim by sound of trumpet —

"THAT THE KING'S SON WOULD MARRY ANY LADY WHO SHOULD BE FOUND ABLE TO WEAR THE GLASS SLIPPER WHICH HAD BEEN DROPPED AT THE BALL."

He had noticed that the unknown lady had a pretty little foot, and felt sure he could by this means discover the owner of the slipper. So the herald went round the city and made the announcement in due form.

There was a great stir, you may be sure; for it was not every day that a chance was offered to marry a Prince. It was noticed that the excitement was greatest among those fair ladies who had small feet, while the many not thus endowed preferred to think the proclamation only a silly joke.

Many a lady tried to make the slipper fit, but in vain; for, you see, it was glass, and would not bend like an ordinary shoe. First one and then another tried, but all were obliged to dismiss the herald, and to renounce their hopes of obtaining the Prince's hand.

At last the herald came to the house of the two sisters. They knew well enough, of course, that neither of themselves was the beautiful lady, but they tried and tried again to get their clumsy feet into the slipper. At last they had to give up.

All this while Cinderella had been quietly listening in the chimney-corner. She now came forward and modestly asked if she might try.

"You!" cried the sisters, bursting into laughter.

"Did anyone ever hear anything so absurd!"

But the herald looked gravely at Cinderella's sweet face, and said his orders were to let anyone who liked to try on the slipper.

So he made Cinderella sit down, the sisters regarding her with an ugly sneer. At the very first attempt the slipper was seen to fit exactly, in fact on Cinderella's dainty little foot it appeared to be a skin of glass.

The sisters looked on, speechless with surprise. Their wonder increased when Cinderella quietly said that she had been at the ball and had danced with the Prince. They looked at each other as if to say, "However could a kitchen-maid have got in?" To convince the herald, Cinderella quietly put her hand in her pocket and drew out the other slipper, which she had carried about ever since the night of the ball.

Now, at last, the sisters began to see in Cinderella's face some likeness to the beautiful lady whose notice they were so proud and happy to attract at the ball; but their wonder was still not yet at an end, for the Fairy Godmother had entered the room unseen and now touched Cinderella with her wand, transforming the humble maiden again into the beautiful and richly dressed Princess who had excited so much admiration at the balls.

The herald, overjoyed with his success, at once returned to the palace to report to the Prince.

You may well imagine the feelings of the sisters. Amazement gave way to alarm, and at last to shame. Falling on their knees, and with tears in their eyes, they begged Cinderella's pardon for all their former unkindness.

But Cinderella was of too fine a character to cherish ill-feeling. She not only freely forgave, but promised to do everything in her power to help them.

Soon the herald returned and she was conducted in state to the royal palace. The Prince was delighted to have found her again, and thought she looked even more beautiful than before. The King and all the court were very much pleased with her story, and soon everybody in the land was expressing a wish that he or she could have a Fairy Godmother.

The wedding took place soon afterwards amid great rejoicings. A special place was reserved for the two sisters, though really they hardly deserved it.

As for Cinderella, she was as happy as the days were long. But, after all, she owed more of her joy to her own sweet and sunny nature and to her kind and loving disposition than to all the good gifts her devoted husband showered upon her.

The cook would often hit Dick on the head with the
frying pan

The King was greatly delighted for he had never seen such a
clever cat before

DICK WHITTINGTON
AND HIS CAT

Many, many years ago in a little English village there lived an orphan lad named Dick Whittington. His mother and father had died when he was very young, and though the folk nearby were kind and did their best for the lonely boy, they were very poor themselves and had little to spare. So, for the most part, he lived on hard crusts and the odds and ends on which the dogs are usually fed.

When Dick had grown to be a big lad, he made up his mind to go to London, for he had heard many wonderful stories of the great City – how the streets were paved with gold, and handsome lords and ladies were as plentiful as acorns – and he felt sure, being a sharp fellow, that once he got there he would quickly make his fortune.

One day, hearing that a wagoner he knew was going to London with fruit and vegetables, he asked the man to find room for him. They had a rough journey, for the weather was very bad, and the deep ruts in the road made the wagon jolt horribly; but Dick was so busy building castles in the air, and thinking of the wonderful things he was going to do, that no discomfort troubled him.

At last they rumbled into the great City; and the kindly wagoner put Dick down in a dingy street and drove off to the market. Dick walked through street after street, expecting every moment to come in sight of the golden pavement, and thinking that he would then only have to break off a piece to have as much money as he wanted. But he saw nothing but narrow, dirty, winding streets that did not please him at all.

All the people who passed seemed too busy even to notice him. He kept on walking, feeling more and more hungry, in the hope of getting food and work somewhere. He saw a few fine lords and pretty ladies, but not a sign of the golden pavement.

At last night came on, and Dick had nowhere to go for shelter, so, being by this time quite worn out, as well as cold and hungry, he crept into the doorway of a large house and soon fell fast asleep.

This house happened to belong to one of the richest merchants of London, Master Fitzwarren. When Dick woke next morning he found some of the merchant's servants standing over him and proposing to have him sent to jail. At this moment the owner of the house came out.

"Why did you lie here, my lad?" asked the merchant in a kind voice.

Dick explained that he had only done so for shelter, and begged so hard to be allowed to do some work that the merchant gave orders that he was to be taken to the kitchen, given a good breakfast, and then set to whatever dirty work the cook required.

Dick worked so well that he was allowed to remain in Master Fitzwarren's house. He would have been quite happy had it not been for the cook, who was a cross old woman and treated him very badly. Often she would hit him on the head with the frying pan and call him all sorts of nasty names. But Dick put up with this ill-treatment because of his master's pretty young daughter, Mistress Alice, who had always a kind word and a smile for him. The footman, too, was good and taught him to read.

One day Dick had a penny given to him by Mistress Alice, and with it he bought a cat from a poor girl, because there were so many rats and mice in the cellar where he slept that they kept him awake at night as they scampered over the floor and across the bed. The cat proved to be a splendid "mouser" and soon cleared all the rats and mice. Dick grew so fond of his pet that he rarely moved without her.

After Dick had lived in the merchant's house for some months, Master Fitzwarren one day called all his servants into the kitchen, and, telling them that he was sending a ship to trade in foreign parts, asked if they would like to send any money or goods, so that the captain might do a little business for them.

All the servants sent something except Dick. Mistress Alice offered to lend him some money for the venture, but the merchant said that this would bring no luck, and Dick must send something of his own or nothing at all.

"But I have nothing but my cat, for which I paid a penny," said Dick woefully.

"Then, send your cat, lad!" said Master Fitzwarren with a laugh.

So Dick, with tearstained eyes, brought his beloved Puss and handed her over to the captain.

"Now I shall be kept awake all night by the rats and mice," he lamented.

At this the captain and all the ship's company laughed, for it seemed a droll idea that a cat should form part of a trading venture.

After the ship had sailed, Dick had a worse time than ever, for the cook grew more ill-tempered and spiteful every day. Now that his cat had gone, and pretty Mistress Alice was away from home, he had no one to comfort him. At last he felt so unhappy that he made up his mind to run away.

Early on the morning of All-Hallow Day he rose and dressed long before anyone else was awake, and, having bundled his few belongings into a handkerchief, crept quietly out of the house, and set off along the Great North Road.

He walked for a long time, feeling very lonely and very miserable, and at last came to Highgate Hill, where he sat on a mile-stone to rest. While he sadly wondered what he should do next, he heard far away the bells of Bow Church; and it seemed as he listened that they were chiming a message meant especially for him:

> *"Turn again, Whittington,*
> *Thrice Lord Mayor of London!"*

"Ah!" thought Dick, "to be Lord Mayor of London would suit me very well. But if I am to be Lord Mayor, I must not run away."

Still he listened to the bells, and again it seemed that they chimed the words:

> *"Turn again, Whittington,*
> *Thrice Lord Mayor of London!"*

His hopes renewed, Dick sprang to his feet and turned his steps again to London Town, feeling sure the future held something good in store for him. He hurried back to the merchant's house, and was just in time to slip into the kitchen as the cross old cook came downstairs, grumbling as usual.

But Dick did not in the least mind the cook's bad temper now; he felt cheerful and happy and did his work so well that no one could find fault with him. Gentle Mistress Alice, when she returned, still smiled on him so sweetly when they met on the stairs that Dick fell hopelessly in love with her, and made up his mind that if ever he did become Lord Mayor of London he would certainly marry her – provided, of course, she would have him, which, somehow, he was bold enough to believe she would.

Meanwhile, the ship, with Dick's precious cat on board, had crossed the seas to the coast of Barbary. Here the captain took his goods on shore to sell to the King of the country.

The King was pleased to buy a number of things, and invited the captain and his chief mate to come back to the palace. Here a grand feast was provided; but just as the dishes were set before the company a fearful swarm of rats and mice ran on to the table and carried off most of the food, scattering pieces of meat all over the room.

The King apologized for these pests, but explained that his land was overrun with them, and that he could never eat a meal in peace. "In fact," he said, "I would give half my treasures to anyone who would rid me of this plague."

The captain at once thought of Dick's cat, and next day, when he again came to dine with the King, be brought Puss with him. Half-way through the meal the rats and mice again scampered on to the table. Instantly the cat sprang from the captain's arms and pounced upon the creatures, killing many and scaring the rest away.

The King was greatly delighted, and declared that he must have the cat at all costs, for he had never seen so wonderful an animal before. In fact, he gladly gave the captain a hundred times as much gold for Dick's cat as for all the other goods put together.

So Puss was left behind in Barbary, to feed on rats and mice to her heart's content, and the captain set sail for England. Soon after landing he returned to Master Fitzwarren's house to render an account of his voyage.

The servants were all called into the kitchen to hear the results of their trading; but the cook told Dick that it was useless for him to go, as "all he would get would be his old black cat again."

When the captain had told the story of the King, and displayed the bags of gold and treasure that had been paid for Dick's cat, the merchant cried, "Why, Dick will be the richest lad in all London!"

The cross cook begged him not to think of giving so much treasure to a mere kitchen boy who would not know what to do with it; but to take a fair portion himself and share the rest among the other servants. But the merchant declared that Dick should have every penny.

So Dick was sent for in a hurry, and came running in with a soup-ladle he was polishing in his hands. He could scarcely believe his eyes when he saw the pile of money-bags and gold plate. The honest merchant refused to take any of the money himself, but invited Dick to stay in the house as his guest until he could find a house suitable for his new degree.

No need to tell you how delighted Dick was with his good fortune. He had looked handsome even as a kitchen boy, but when the tailor had made him a costly suit of rich velvet, Mistress Alice vowed that she had never seen a better man, and it was not long before he persuaded her to be his bride.

As the years passed, Dick traded with his fortune, and grew richer and richer; and the message of the bells of Bow Church came true, for he was thrice Lord Mayor of London (some people say four times) and was made a Knight.

At one of the splendid banquets he gave, he was graced by the presence of King Henry the Fifth; and, knowing that the King was greatly in need of money for the war in France, he offered him the whole of his fortune.

The King gladly accepted a portion only, and exclaimed gratefully, "Never had Prince such a subject!"

To which Sir Richard replied very gallantly, "Never had subject such a Prince!"

Sir Richard lived on, happy and respected to the end of his days. Remembering his own early years, he was always very good to the poor, and if ever you go to the Royal Exchange, in London, you will see a fine picture which shows him dispensing his charities. We may be pretty sure also that he was always good to cats.

BLUEBEARD

nce upon a time there lived in an Eastern city a merchant named Abdullah, who had lost so many ships and had so many misfortunes that, try as he would, he seemed to grow poorer and poorer. As soon as he had put by a little money he was sure to lose it all in his next venture.

Abdullah felt his bad fortune all the more because he had a family to keep. His son, Hassan, could look after himself; but it made the merchant sad to think that he could not provide for his two young daughters.

These daughters were both very pretty; but the younger one was the prettiest girl in all the town. Her name was Fatima, and she had eyes as black as sloe berries and hair that shone like the wings of a raven.

The elder daughter, Anne, was also a very charming girl, and the two loved each other so dearly that they could not bear to be separated. Although their father had been so unfortunate, he had contrived that his girls should be well brought up, and taught to dance and sing, and to behave in becoming fashion. But they had never known the joy of wearing fine clothes and rich jewels to set off their beauty.

One day, when things were at their worst with Abdullah, and it seemed that no good fortune could possibly attend him, a rich stranger called to see him.

The stranger was very gorgeously dressed in a flowing silk robe of brilliant colours and wore chains of dazzling jewels. But there was one very curious and remarkable thing about him. His long beard, instead of being black, or brown, or ginger, or white, like other men's, was of a bright blue shade, and for this reason he was known by the name of BLUEBEARD.

Abdullah was greatly surprised to see this wealthy stranger; but he was still more surprised when Bluebeard presently declared that he desired to marry his beautiful daughter, Fatima.

"I have seen the maiden," he said. "I like her pretty looks, and, if she will marry me, she shall wear the finest of clothes and live grandly in a palace like a princess!"

Abdullah said that he would find out what his daughter thought about the matter, and told Bluebeard to call for his answer on the following day.

When Fatima heard the news, she cried in alarm,

"What! Marry a man with an ugly blue beard. Not I."

But her father begged her to think how splendid it would be to live like a princess, and how much she could help him in his present troubles by marrying so rich a man. Fatima, who loved her father dearly, thus came to think it was her duty to consent. Besides, she loved pretty clothes and fine jewels, and she certainly felt it would be nice to live in a palace.

So, when the next morning Bluebeard called for an answer, Fatima agreed to marry him. "But," said she, "my dear sister Anne must come with me, for I will never be separated from her!"

Many bridegrooms would have objected to this, but Bluebeard proved most obliging and readily consented. The wedding took place a few days afterwards.

When the day came for her to leave home Fatima wept, for she could not conceal from herself that she did not like the appearance of her husband, and was in fear of him. But her brother Hassan called her aside and promised that he would follow in a few days to see that all was well with her.

Then Bluebeard took Fatima and Anne to his palace, which was some distance out in the country. At first the two sisters were delighted with their new life; the palace was splendid; they had slaves to wait upon their slightest wish; and there seemed no end to the fine robes and beautiful jewels they were free to wear whenever they pleased.

But soon they discovered that Bluebeard was really a very cruel and wicked man. He still continued to treat them fairly, but they were very glad when one day he announced that he was going away for a few days.

Before leaving, he handed to Fatima the keys of the palace, saying that she might use them all and go wherever she pleased. One key, however, she was not to use. It was a little one which fitted the door of a chamber which was always kept locked.

"If you open that door," said Bluebeard, "I shall be very angry indeed, and will certainly cut off your head!"

A few hours later Bluebeard took his departure, and Fatima and Anne were left in charge.

They spent several days roaming over the beautiful palace, with its wealth of wonders, and went into every room except that which had been forbidden to them. Then, having little else to occupy their minds, they began to wonder more and more what could be hidden in this mysterious chamber. The more they thought about it, the more curious they became.

At last, one day, Fatima said, "Let us take just one peep within! We can easily lock the door again, and Bluebeard cannot possibly know! After all, why shouldn't we look?"

Sister Anne agreed and, after some trouble, they fitted the key into the lock of the secret chamber, and turned it.

The door at once flew open, and the key fell upon the floor. Then the two sisters shrieked with horror at the sight that met their eyes. On the wall at the back they saw a long row of maidens' heads, each hanging from a hook by means of its own hair, and the floor was stained with the blood of the wretched victims!

Fatima nearly fainted with fright at this fearful sight, but Anne hurriedly dragged her from this chamber of horrors and locked the door again.

The two sisters now knew beyond a doubt that Bluebeard was a cruel and wicked wretch who enticed fair maidens to marry him and then killed them without mercy as soon as he grew tired of them.

They quickly resolved, while there was yet time, to seek safety in flight.

But this proved to be the very day of Bluebeard's return. Even as they spoke he entered the palace and, a few moments later, came into the room. Having glanced round suspiciously he asked for the keys, and